Bully
-Be-
Gone

THE MISADVENTURES OF
Millicent Madding

Bully
-Be-
Gone

BRIAN TACANG

HarperCollins*Publishers*

The Misadventures of Millicent Madding #1:

Bully-Be-Gone

www.harperchildrens.com

Library of Congress Cataloging-in-Publication Data

Tacang, Brian.

Bully-be-gone / Brian Tacang.— 1st ed.

p. cm.—(The misadventures of Millicent Madding ; #1)

Summary: Budding inventor Millicent Madding launches her latest invention to disastrous results, and she has only days to create an antidote before the local bullies wreak havoc and her dearest friendships are destroyed forever.

ISBN-10: 0-06-073911-8 (trade bdg.)

ISBN-13: 978-0-06-073911-9 (trade bdg.)

ISBN-10: 0-06-073912-6 (lib. bdg.)

ISBN-13: 978-0-06-073912-6 (lib. bdg.)

[1. Bullies—Fiction. 2. Inventors—Fiction. 3. Libraries—Fiction. 4. Friendship—Fiction. 5. Humorous stories.]

I. Title. II. Series.

PZ7.T1156Bul 200   2005007777

[Fic]—dc22   CIP

                                                                          AC

Typography by Sasha Illingworth

1 2 3 4 5 6 7 8 9 10

First Edition

This book is dedicated to
Linda Watanabe McFerrin, Goddess of Language,
and to Justin, Sustainer of All Things Good.

Special thanks to:
The No Coast Writers past and present (Susan, Susan, Susan, Suzy, Steve, Bonnie, Bunny, Martha, Madeleine, Monique, Kyra, Karin, and Emily—what a talented group, not to mention alliteratively fun), the Life into Literature writers (my original gang, which includes: Susan, Anjin, Mary Brent, Lori, Kathryn, Jean, Marianne, Lenny, Kara, and Kevin), Julie Johns (my best and highest leaping cheerleader), Maggie Lichtenberg (whose workshop helped me to finish this book), Joe Veltre (to whom I owe more than his percentage covers), Leann Heywood (a great editor who makes me think a little bit harder), and my entire family who, since my first steps, never stopped clapping. Finally, I'd like to thank all of the bullies in my life (corporate and otherwise) who, inadvertently, helped me to become more of who I am.

If I could do it all over again, I would change only one minor detail of my life. I would still have begun my career sitting on my head and I would still have ended it bent over backward. Ah, but the in-between? That mysterious, glorious middle period? For all of its joys, its triumphs, its horrible mistakes, I would have paid closer attention.

—Winifred T. Langley,
a.k.a. the Bendable Francine Tippit

Prologue

Millicent poured a vial of clear liquid into the beaker of milky liquid. A layer of white fizz formed, but quickly settled. She hadn't expected that reaction and hissed a quiet, "whew." Thank goodness it hadn't exploded.

She checked the clock nearby. Midnight. She rubbed her eyes and yawned.

To her right sat three bottles of gels and liquids, each a different shade of blue, waiting to be added to the mixture. She took the first one, a turquoise memory-jogging gel she'd concocted, and added it to the beaker. Then she poured in a bit from the second bottle, a blend of every happy smell known to humankind she called Blissaroma.

Millicent yawned again. "I am so tired," she murmured as she poured a little more Blissaroma into the beaker.

Referring to her notes, she squinted and tried to focus on her scribbled formula. Her printing looked blurry, as if it were moving across the paper like ballroom dancers on a white marble floor. She knew her next and final ingredient was her Propulsion Lotion, but she couldn't quite read how much to use. She rubbed her eyes. When she printed, she made her periods look like little *o*'s. *Is that Propulsion Lotion: 1. milliliter? Or 10 milliliters?*

She measured out what she thought was the correct amount and added it to the beaker. Bang! A small explosion blew her bangs straight into the air, as if she'd just entered a wind tunnel.

"Yikes!"

She wiped her forehead with the sleeve of her lab coat and retied her braids, which had come undone. She swirled the beaker around for a few seconds, then placed it on a Bunsen burner. When the blue liquid bubbled to almost overflowing, she removed the beaker. While the concoction cooled and thickened, she prepared several bottles, plastic deodorant applicators, and foil packets.

When the beaker reached room temperature, she mixed some of the thick blue substance with a waxy deodorant base and some of it with her own special sunscreen formula. She put both blends into their respective containers, Finally, she injected the remaining gel into foil envelopes.

"There," she said, admiring her line of products, their blue labels staring back at her like an enthusiastic audience. She tipped her chair back and clasped her hands behind her head. Madame Curie, her golden Abyssinian cat, leaped from the floor to the lab table.

"What do you think, M.C.?" Millicent asked the cat, nudging a bottle toward her. "My best invention ever. Just in time for the new school year."

The cat sniffed at the bottle and jutted out her chin, which gave her a cynical air, a standard facial expression for an Abyssinian cat. She seemed to be thinking, *Smells to me like another dud.*

"Oh, ye cat of little faith," Millicent said, squeezing the cat's chin gently between her thumb and forefinger. She held a blue bottle up to the light with her free hand, turning it so that it sparkled. "This will guarantee that my friends and I will never be picked on again." She sighed and added, "I hope."

She yawned. "I'll just rest my eyes," she said, laying her head on her notebook. "Just . . . rest . . . for . . . a . . . bit." In seconds, she was asleep.

Outside, night had swallowed the house. The stars winked at Millicent as she slept on her notebook. The moon smiled at her and the streetlights beamed good fortune.

It had all the makings of a lucky night—except for the crickets, who were laughing hysterically.

One

A knock at the laboratory door woke Millicent. She sat up and felt the side of her face. The spiral binding of her notebook had left ridges down her cheek.

"Millicent," said her uncle through the door. "Fell asleep down here again, eh?"

"Yeah, Uncle Phineas."

"Product launch today. Yes, yes. Exciting."

"I know, Uncle Phineas," she replied. "I know." Last night, she had been filled with excitement as she completed her latest invention. But this morning, the mere mention of her product launch made her stomach feel as though it had been shaken by a paint mixer at the hardware store.

"Hmmm. You sound nervous," Uncle Phineas said. "No need for it, yes. Half the formula is effort, half is belief in yourself. Yes, yes. Well . . ." His voice grew faint as he shuffled back up the stairs.

"Geez," she said, rubbing her eyes and looking around the lab.

Millicent and her guardian, Phineas Baldernot, shared the bottom floor of the house as their work space, otherwise referred to as Baldernot Madding Laboratories.

Uncle Phineas had renovated the entire basement many years ago, installing a network of sinks, tables, desks, and cabinets. He'd provided Millicent with every gadget and contrivance she would ever need to hone her skills as an inventor.

She had her own corner desk, five computers, and a granite-topped worktable, complete with a stainless steel sink. Metal cabinets lined one wall, each under lock and key. Millicent was free to use whatever chemicals, tools, or other materials she wanted from within the cabinets as long as she registered what she took on a master clipboard hanging from the middle cabinet.

Millicent liked the arrangement. And she liked working closely with Uncle Phineas. He didn't peer over her shoulder and bombard her with advice. He treated her as an associate, not as a little girl. Even when she'd ask for his input on a particular combination of chemicals or a certain junction of wires, he'd bend over and peer into her eyes.

"What do you think will happen?" he'd ask. A question to which she didn't always have an answer.

Whatever gadget or potion she invented, Uncle Phineas had only one requirement—that it improve someone's life, even if it were in the smallest way. He said the desire to make people's lives better was the hallmark of all great inventors.

Millicent looked up at the ceiling. "Good morning, everyone," she said, trying to muster a cheerful tone. A league of Masonville's most respected inventors and scientists stared back at her.

They were posters of her idols. Among them, a large photo of Inga Wymeronner, inventor of the PetLepathy Collar, a small screen your dog wore around his neck that showed his barks translated into English.

A few pictures of Bramwell Phitt, inventor of the Calorie Thermometer, a wallet-sized tool folks used to count their calories by sticking it in their food, were also sprinkled around the ceiling.

Mostly, though, huge posters of Uncle Phineas dotted the ceiling. His most popular invention, a hair growth tonic called Diffollicle Speed Gel, was available in curly, straight, or kinky formulas and in a variety of colors. With it, you could completely change your hair's color and texture from the roots. Each of the posters of Uncle Phineas was different. One showed him with long, red, wavy locks, another with a blond afro, another with a black pageboy—all worn with his signature bushy white beard.

A huge metal box, as black as a black hole and as large as a walk-in closet, stood in one corner of the lab. It had a row of lights on top and a large red dial to the right of its front door. The words MILLENNIUM TRAVEL CUBE were engraved above the door. Taped on the door was Millicent's favorite picture, that of her parents, Adair and Astrid Madding.

Adair and Astrid were inventors, too. Together, they were responsible for a series of fine inventions from Espresso Toothpaste—for busy people with no time to grab a cup of coffee, let alone brush their teeth—to the Lint Knitter Dryer, a clothes dryer that knitted scarves, socks, and beanies from leftover fibers in the lint catcher.

But their one failed invention, the black metal box in the corner, loomed like a sad memory. It was their most ambitious invention and could have been their greatest.

Millicent got off her lab stool and went over to the Millennium Travel Cube. She stood there, staring at her parents' picture. She reached toward the cube and ran her hand along the smooth surface of the door, letting it linger near the latch. "I could use a little help. I'm really anxious," she said to the picture.

In the photo, her mom and dad looked as cheerful as the day they went away. Millicent was barely six when they had stepped into the Millennium Travel Cube. "Time travel, the wave of the future," her mom had said before entering the cube. "We'll be back shortly," said her dad before shutting the cube's door. They were never seen again.

For months after they disappeared, Millicent used to

knock on the Travel Cube's door saying, "Mommy? Daddy? Are you in there? Come out now. Please." Sometimes, she'd fall asleep at the door, swaddled in her favorite blanket. When she was older—eight or nine years old—she would tinker with the Travel Cube, hoping to get her mom and dad back. Uncle Phineas even tried helping her—to no avail. The Travel Cube was far too complex, its codes too complicated for either of them to crack. She often wondered where in time her parents were and what they were doing. Were they dining with Julia Child? Dancing with Josephine Baker? Painting with Frida Kahlo? Or were their journeys local? Were they hanging out with Masonville's own historic figures: Ellery Winkery, inventor of the prosthetic eyelid, or Hannah Ovver, the famed three-armed xylophonist? Wherever they were, the Travel Cube was a constant reminder they weren't here. Nowadays, Millicent regarded the Travel Cube as a dare. She wasn't yet ready to tackle it. One day, though, she'd be ready. In the meantime, Millicent often found comfort in talking to her parents' picture when she had a problem.

"You see, Mom and Dad," Millicent said, "I've got another product I've been working on all summer. I'm launching it at the Wunderkind Club meeting today."

The Wunderkind Club, a collection of the best and brightest students at Winifred T. Langley Middle School, held monthly meetings in which they shared their talents and accomplishments, safe from the teasing of their less-accomplished fellow students. Millicent used to introduce her new inventions at these meetings. However, she hadn't introduced anything in a long time.

"I haven't had a successful invention in nearly a year," she said. "The last one? The Automatic Ponytail Retractor? A dismal failure."

Anita Ferratta, Millicent's best customer, had worn the Automatic Ponytail Retractor, designed to keep girls' ponytails out of the hands of mischievous boys, on her head. Disguised as a feathered headband, it had a cluster of gears and metal claws in back, through which Anita had threaded her ponytail. A pesky boy, who sat behind her in science class, was about to yank her ponytail. Anita saw him in the miniature rearview mirror—a bonus feature of the Automatic Ponytail Retractor—and hit the emergency button. Something went terribly wrong with the rewind mechanism. There was a horrible whirring and clicking, like a broken grandfather clock going backward in time. The machine sucked up Anita's ponytail, leaving it in a tangled clump that eventually had to be cut from her head.

The now boyish-looking Anita stopped speaking to Millicent. And that hurt her more than if Anita had gotten angry and yelled at her.

"So you can see why I'm nervous," she said to her mom and dad. "It's not like I can afford to lose any more friends due to a crummy invention."

Millicent glanced at the top of her granite worktable, where several bottles of the cobalt-blue liquid sat. Even though the bottles were pretty, Millicent knew their beauty alone wouldn't cut it with the Wunderkind Club. The Wunderkinder had seen more than their share of her potions and gadgets. And with each one that failed, she lost a little more of her friends' respect.

"Hey, Mom and Dad, will you listen to this and let me know if it sounds okay?" she asked. "It's my sales pitch. Ready?"

According to Uncle Phineas, a pitch was an artful sales talk, a means of getting customers interested in your product. He said pitching your product was an important step to the final sale. He said you could never practice a pitch enough. And pitches had to be catchy and dramatic and a little bit corny. He would know. He pitched his products all the time. Her parents used to pitch their products, too.

"Fellow Wunderkinder," Millicent began. "There is a word for the kind of student that strikes fear in our hearts." Here, she paused for effect. She began her next sentence in a hiss and ended in a shout, her finger pointed at the ceiling. "They lurk in the halls, hide in the bathrooms, are sorry victims of trendy attire, and listen to music with poorly rhymed lyrics."

She took a step forward. "Then I'll ask, 'Do you know what that word is?' Before any of them has the chance to answer, I'll say, 'Bully.' The word is 'bully.'"

Nice, she imagined her mom saying.

She folded her arms across her chest.

"A number of disruptive things could happen at this point," she said to her parents' picture. "But I'm prepared.

Don't worry. I can't afford to let things get out of hand."

True, she could hear her dad saying.

Millicent paced in front of the Millennium Travel Cube.

"I expect a wordy response from Tonisha Fontaine," she said.

Your best friend, her mom said.

"And a poet," Millicent added. "She has the very annoying habit of writing down everything you say in a spiral-bound notepad. Then she edits what you said and adds a few words of her own. She calls it poetry. Well, she does make your words sound somewhat better than when you said them, I'll give her that much. Simplicity works best with Tonisha—the fewer words you speak, the fewer you give her to rewrite—so I'll just have to nab her pen."

That's our girl, her dad said.

Millicent put her hand to her chin, thinking. "But—"

Yes? her parents asked.

"I'm most worried about Roderick Biggleton."

Roderick Biggleton, her parents mulled. *Is he the—*

"Third . . . of the West Side Biggletons," Millicent answered.

I remember the Biggleton clan, said her dad. *Barracudas.*

"That's them," Millicent agreed. "Roderick's father is Roderick Biggleton the Second, the well-known corporate attorney. His mother, Eloise Biggleton, is the glamorous owner and president of Beauty Goo Cosmetics. Her mottoes are plastered on nearly every billboard and bus stop in town."

Oh, wait! said her mom. *I remember them: 'Goo for You,*

*Feel Goo About Yourself, Goo Things Come in Small Packages,'
and 'Goo Things Come to Those Who Wait,' to name a few.* Her
mother winked. *I always thought they were snappy.*

"We're talking about Roderick Biggleton, Mom. I'm
worried that Roderick will turn everyone against me before
I have the chance to sell my product. I'll have to be super
clever with him."

She waited for her dad to say something.

"Well, what do you think?" she asked the picture.

"I think you'll be late, yes," a voice said.

Millicent nearly jumped three feet into the air. "Uncle
Phineas!" she gasped.

Uncle Phineas approached her from behind, put his
hand on her shoulder, and lowered his face so that his
cheek pressed against hers. "I'm sure they can hear you
from wherever they are."

Millicent squinted at him doubtfully.

"I talk to my Felicity daily," he said.

Millicent had seen him talk to Aunt Felicity's pictures—
dozens of them—that he'd placed around the house, as if
he might forget her between walking from the living room
to the kitchen. Millicent always thought he looked terribly
sad talking to her pictures.

Uncle Phineas straightened up. "The language of the
heart . . . there's no telling how far that can travel, yes?"

"Maybe," Millicent said, dragging the toe of her shoe
across the concrete floor. "But what good does it do if
everyone leaves?"

"Abandonment, dear niece, is a matter of perspective," Uncle Phineas said. "If people leave but stay in your mind, have they really left? Speaking of leaving, you should be getting ready."

Millicent looked at the lab clock. Nine o'clock. She had exactly one hour to get ready, gather her presentation materials, and make her grand entrance at the Wunderkind Club meeting, the last one of the summer. She took a deep breath, then rushed upstairs to shower and dress.

Breakfast was ready when she entered the kitchen: English muffins, two scrambled eggs, and hash browns.

Uncle Phineas futzed with the toaster, screwdriver in hand. This morning his hair was curly and brown.

"Apologies for the English muffins, Millicent," he said with his back to her. "Toaster is on the blink, yes." He turned to face her. "Could be because I've made it into the Morning News Toaster."

Millicent sat down at the table. Her English muffins looked okay; golden edges on every crater. She turned one over, exposing its blackened underside. She turned the other over. It was pasty white and soft underneath.

"The English muffins are fine," she said, reaching for the butter. "Morning News Toaster?"

"Certainly. When would one listen to the news but when one is making toast, yes?" he said. "How did you order your muffins? Medium? Light? Dark?"

"I didn't order English muffins," she answered. "I ordered cereal."

"Odd," he said. "'English muffins' and 'cereal' sound nothing alike. I'll have to check the connection between the Robotic Chef and the Morning News Toaster. Yes, yes."

Uncle Phineas had invented the Robotic Chef System for his wife, Felicity. Although she had disappeared many years ago, Uncle Phineas kept the system in relatively good working order since he couldn't cook at all.

"Everything else is perfect," Millicent said, pushing her food around on her plate with her fork.

She didn't have the heart to tell him she hadn't ordered eggs or hash browns either.

"There," Uncle Phineas said, tapping his screwdriver on the counter. He put a piece of bread in the toaster and pressed the lever. The morning news came on immediately.

"In breaking news," the radio newscaster said, "the Mega-Stupenda Mart is reporting that three top-of-the-line bicycles were stolen this morning."

"Well," Uncle Phineas mumbled.

"Descriptions of the three robbers are sketchy," the newscaster continued. "Seen by witnesses only fleetingly, and in silhouette, they are described as 'one tall, one short and heavy, and one with incredibly long arms.' They are believed to be youngsters. Anyone with information regarding the robbery is encouraged to contact the Masonville police."

Millicent was only half listening to the news report. Her

upcoming presentation dominated her thoughts. "Ketchup on my eggs, please," Millicent said into the Robotic Chef's microphone located in the middle of the kitchen table.

The refrigerator opened and a metal arm reached out, a bottle in its steel grip. A red sensor on its wrist scanned her plate for scrambled eggs. It poured syrup on her hash browns.

Close enough, she thought.

"Can you believe that? Stealing bikes? In broad daylight?" Uncle Phineas asked.

"Ridiculous," Millicent answered while cutting her food.

"And a threesome of youngsters, no less," he commented.

"A threesome," she echoed, popping a wad of eggs into her mouth.

"Raising young people is a baffling job," Uncle Phineas said. "Too much discipline and they rebel. Not enough and they run rampant. I confess, I make it up as I go."

"I think you do pretty well," Millicent said. Ever since Uncle Phineas became her guardian, he'd measured out his authority only when Millicent had truly deserved it.

"Say, Millicent, would you like to see my latest creation? Yes?" Uncle Phineas asked, waving his screwdriver.

"Sure," she said, perking up. She set down her utensils. Uncle Phineas oozed inspiration.

"What do you do if you're waiting in a long line, at the post office, say, and you want to sit?" he asked.

She knew that pitches included compelling questions

16

meant to engage customers. She played along by answering with another question.

"Get out of line?" she asked.

"You could," said Uncle Phineas. "Unless you were wearing Phineas's Inflatable Chair Pants!"

A deafening gust of wind came from beneath Uncle Phineas's white lab coat. Millicent covered her mouth in shock and, for a second, she thought he really ought to excuse himself. He turned around, revealing an inflatable chair sticking out of his trousers. He sat down and crossed his legs.

"As you can see," he said smugly, "there's no place that's not a sitting place with Phineas's Inflatable Chair Pants."

A high-pitched whistle pierced the air, like that of a punctured raft, but Uncle Phineas ignored it.

"The convenience of furniture, the tailoring of an Italian suit," he said, his arms outstretched.

He sank farther and farther with each word.

"Uncle Phineas," she said.

"A chair for anywhere," he said.

"Uncle Phineas!" she said more urgently.

"Standing room only?" he asked. "Not so with—Oh, dear."

Uncle Phineas lay on the floor on a mat of plastic. Millicent leaped to help him up.

"It's a great idea, Uncle Phineas," she said, struggling to get him to his feet.

"Yes, yes. Well—" he said, standing and brushing himself off. "Minor problem. Utterly fixable."

"Without a doubt," she said.

"Indeed," he said. "And your invention? Launching today, eh?"

"Yeah," she said, tilting her head downward. She felt nervous all over again.

"What's wrong, Love?" he asked, stooping and placing his arm around her shoulders.

"I'm worried," said Millicent. "Worried it won't work."

Uncle Phineas placed his hand under her chin and lifted her head until her face was fully lit by the morning sun streaming through the window.

"Nothing is ever perfect," he said. "That's why we invent. Imperfect inventions for an imperfect world. We inventors do little more than create the illusion of perfection. If we're lucky, there'll be a brief, flawless moment in the whole mess. And if we're especially lucky, we'll be partly responsible for it."

Millicent poked at her eggs.

"Not convinced, eh?"

"I only hope you're right," she said.

"Faith, my dear niece," he said. "Faith, science, and a little finger crossing."

Millicent looked at him, his curly brown hair of the day, his white beard, his green eyes. She wanted to believe him. She had the science and finger crossing down. What she needed to muster between now and the Wunderkind Club meeting was at least a beaker full of faith.

Two

During the summer, the Wunderkind Club gathered at the Masonville public library in a secret room. The room was concealed behind an immense iron door which, in turn, was concealed behind a bookcase in the children's book section. Only the Wunderkinder and a few select others knew of the room's existence.

In the mid-seventeen hundreds, Millicent's great-great-great-great grandmother Goody Constance Madding founded the Masonville public library.

Goody Madding loved books—the smell of their leather bindings, the rustle of their pages, their printed wisdom.

And she loved collecting them. Because of her, Masonville's library enjoyed the reputation of being the most well-stocked library in the region. Her life would have been utterly fulfilled were it not for a certain organization bent on enforcing its will in Masonville's every nook and cranny.

The organization went by the name Citizens Loathing Outlandish, Uncivilized Tomes, or CLOUT for short. CLOUT was comprised of needle-lipped, pill-eyed residents with not much to occupy their time or their minds. CLOUT's mission was to identify and eliminate any and all books with which they took issue.

One day, Goody Madding caught wind of a treacherous plot CLOUT was hatching to rid Masonville of a bunch of books they didn't like. She heard the rumor from Goody Akasha Fontaine, a servant who overheard it while cleaning a CLOUT member's home. Goody Fontaine told Goody Madding that CLOUT planned to raid the library in a week.

CLOUT's goal was to burn every book written by authors with strange names. Especially authors with hard-to-pronounce foreign names. After the book burning, CLOUT planned on hosting a party—an all-you-could-eat whole wheat cracker and warm water social—to celebrate.

Goody Madding was horrified. She stood to lose most of her beloved book inventory to CLOUT's bonfire. As she dwelled on it, her horror turned to rage.

Good and mad, Goody Madding mounted her own resistance.

Armed only with a trowel and a tin pail, for seven days straight she dug a room under the library in the wee hours every morning. She lined the finished room with bricks and mortar and filled it with the books CLOUT wanted to destroy. At its entrance, she installed an iron door.

Her crowning invention was a wheeled bookcase on tracks she could push in front of the iron door. CLOUT wouldn't think to look behind the bookcase.

Book burning day came, and the members of CLOUT congregated in the library's portico in a mass of black wool serge and buckled shoes and lit torches. At their lead were three hard-looking villagers. First was Mr. Hatch Farnsworth, the county tax collector, a tall skinny man with mean features. Next was Mr. Fenwick Jones, a pig farmer. He snorted a lot. Third was Goody Agatha Kwaikowski, the local judge and a glove maker with extremely long arms. She held her torch just a little higher than everyone else. On the count of three, CLOUT burst through the library doors. To their dismay, they saw most of the books were gone.

They hunted down Goody Madding, their torchlight dancing ghoulish shadows across the empty bookcases. They found her in the reference section, thumbing through a dictionary. Forming a crescent around her, they shouted, "Goody Madding! Where are those evil books?" Goody Madding smiled and shrugged her shoulders so high they touched the rim of her crisp bonnet. "It beateth me," she said. "They seeming vanished into thin air. Prithee, oh prudent

LOUT members, were you of a mind to actually read them?" Her smart-alecky answer got them hot under their starched white collars. They tied her up and whisked her away to the village meetinghouse.

Goody Madding was put on trial. The CLOUT members charged her with the practice of a darker art than book collecting. Magic. Dematerialization of books.

The outcome shone clear enough for Goody Madding to see. She was going to be found guilty, regardless of her innocence. The jury included Hatch Farnsworth and Fenwick Jones. Goody Agatha Kwaikowski was the judge, her gavel sawn off to a nub to keep her from missing the table entirely when she banged it—her arm was that long. Throughout the trial, Goody Madding said nothing. She did not tell them where the books were hidden or about the secret door. She neither denied nor admitted the use of witchcraft. Instead, when questioned, she repeatedly said, "My only crime, if it is a crime, is my love of books."

CLOUT members had their all-you-could-eat whole wheat cracker and warm water social after all. After they burned Goody Madding at the stake. They never did find out about the secret room or the missing books.

Each successor to Goody Madding's post as librarian has guarded the secret of the room, keeping it in strictest confidence with every generation of Maddings, down to Millicent herself, because they'd inherited the key.

The library was a full seven blocks from Millicent's house. Seeing as she was running a tad late, she was glad she owned a car. Millicent wasn't old enough to drive a real car, but she had an electric car, a miniature version of a sport utility vehicle, given to her by Uncle Phineas.

She loaded her backpack, easel, and flip chart into the back of the car, tying them down to the roll bar with a length of bungee cord to ensure they wouldn't blow away. She started the car. She couldn't have asked for a better driving day. A few wisps of clouds trailed across the sky like faraway flags, and the sun sat as squat as a bag of gold.

She sped down the sidewalk of Dolby Lane, turned left on Tattersall Street, thinking the whole way about her invention.

She was passing Grainy Bits Granary when three figures on bicycles veered into her path and skidded to a stop. She brought her car to an abrupt halt to avoid colliding with them. *Who would be so reckless* . . . she thought, trying to focus on the people in her way. Sunlight flashed off the bicycles into her eyes. She made a visor of her hand, placing it on her forehead.

"Where are you going, nerd?" asked one figure.

She knew that voice. It belonged to Fletch Farnsworth, one of the notorious bully threesome that tormented her and her friends. Fletch dismounted his bike, flicking the kickstand down with his foot. He sauntered toward Millicent, his tall, vulturelike body casting jagged shadows across Millicent's car.

Stopping just shy of her car door, he ran his hand through

his unruly blond hair. "So?" he asked. "Where are you going?"

Millicent trembled. Why hadn't she applied her new product? She wanted to slap her own temple in disgust.

"Going to play with your dorky friends?"

She recognized this froglike croak as Pollywog Jones's voice. Pollywog got off his bike, too, though more awkwardly than Fletch had, his oval face grimacing with the effort. He waddled over to her car, hiking up his pants. Pollywog's waistband often hovered around his full hips like one of Saturn's rings.

"Dorkus," he said, kicking her car. He scratched his baseball cap, which slid back, exposing a fringe of brown hair. "What do I do now?" he asked the third person.

"Move," said the figure.

Nina "the Knuckle" Kwaikowski came into view. Nina slid off her bike, towering before Millicent, her lengthy arms and big hands dangling at her sides like nooses. She put her foot on Millicent's fender.

"Picture it," said Nina, pumping her leg, making Millicent's car bounce like a bucking bronco, "all those weirdos in the same place."

"Oooo," crooned Pollywog. "Let's do multiplication for fun."

"Do a historic time line for kicks," said Fletch, circling Millicent's car.

An *historic time line*, thought Millicent.

"Read a encyclopedia to kill time," said Nina.

"*An* encyclopedia," Millicent said under her breath.

Though she was scared, she couldn't help but correct sloppy grammar. "It's *an* encyclopedia. 'An' almost always precedes a word that starts with the letter 'h' or a vowel. Like *an* imbecile, for example."

"What did you say?" asked Nina.

"Nothing," Millicent said quietly.

"I think she called you a imbecile," said Pollywog to Nina.

An, an, an, thought Millicent, rolling her eyes discreetly.

"That had better be a compliment," said Nina.

In this case it is, thought Millicent.

"This is boring," said Fletch. "Let's ride our bikes down to the ocean."

Yes, please.

"New bikes, new bikes, gotta ride the new bikes," sang Pollywog.

Nina gave Millicent's car one last push with her foot, which made it bounce clear off the pavement. Then she squatted near the driver's side door. She reached a long arm, like a tentacle, into the car and grabbed Millicent by the collar.

"Freak," said Nina, staring into Millicent's eyes.

She tugged Millicent closer—close enough for Millicent to see she hadn't brushed her teeth. Millicent held her breath.

"Yeah, freak," said Pollywog.

Fletch said nothing. He surveyed the area, as if he were being observed.

Nina pulled harder on Millicent's collar. "See you and your mutant friends in school next week," she snarled. "Or sooner," she added with an evil upturn of her mouth. Finally, she released her grip. "C'mon, let's go," she said to Pollywog and Fletch.

The bullies mounted their sparkling bikes. Millicent watched as they pedaled toward Masonville Bay until the glare off their rides became a flicker. Hadn't Uncle Phineas said something about bikes during breakfast? Or perhaps she'd heard mention of bikes on the radio. *Yes!* She thought, *the radio!* She remembered the Mega-Stupenda Mart bike robbery and the descriptions of the robbers. Were the bullies the bike bandits? They certainly fit the profiles, but to be certain, she'd have to get a closer look at their bikes. She needed proof. Half a block away, the trio stopped. Nina motioned with her arm and they made a right turn toward the Masonville public library.

Millicent took a deep breath and shivered. *No*, she thought, *the library is the last place they'd visit*. Just in case, she reached into her backpack and withdrew a bottle of her new product and smeared a patch on her forehead and cheeks, massaging until she felt certain her skin had absorbed the blue lotion.

This new invention had to be launched without a hitch. Though she dreaded another confrontation with the bullies, if it did happen, she'd at least have a success story to share with the Wunderkinder. "Wunderkinder," she'd say, "I have irrefutable evidence my product repels thugs."

She restarted her car, hoping against hope she wouldn't wind up being her own guinea pig.

Three

Guinea pigs are timid-eyed, nervous-nosed creatures, prone to freezing or fleeing at the slightest hint of danger. Millicent bore an uncanny resemblance to one of the edgy rodents when she saw Fletch's, Pollywog's, and Nina's glittering bikes parked on the library's front steps. Her eyes went round and her nose went into spasms of twitching as she pulled up to the building.

She cut the engine and touched her forehead and cheeks to reassure herself. Her face was still tacky from the lotion. She exhaled a burst of air.

"I suppose there's no better way to see if it works," she

said to herself, trying not to hyperventilate. "Deep breaths, deep breaths."

She stepped out of the car and slung her backpack over her shoulder. Next, she unleashed her flip chart and easel, nestling the bulky things as best she could under her arm. She stuck the bungee cord in her backpack and trundled toward the library entrance.

Before entering, she pressed her face against the main door's heavy glass pane. The bullies were nowhere to be seen.

Maybe I can make it to the chamber undetected, she thought, her line of vision slicing a path through the fiction section, past the nonfiction section, clear to the children's room at the rear of the library.

The worst possible outcome would be if the bullies followed her and discovered the Wunderkind Club meeting place.

For several years, the Wunderkinder had been able to keep the location of their meeting chamber a secret. Only the nearsighted, muscular librarian, Miss Ogelvie, knew of its existence.

From a distance, Miss Ogelvie appeared like any other librarian—bespectacled and prudent. Closer inspection revealed that Miss Ogelvie had, through years of lifting books, developed a rather intimidating frame. Her arms, especially, were thick and strong—a fact she played up by having had them tattooed with the faces of literary figures like Shakespeare and Toni Morrison.

Millicent hoped to not attract her attention because,

beyond all else, Miss Ogelvie demanded a quiet library and would lecture anyone who made even the slightest noise.

Millicent strapped the flip chart to her back with the bungee cord, using it as one might a big rubber belt, opened the door, and walked through. The door glided shut, wedging itself between Millicent and her flip chart, sealing Millicent neatly inside the library and her flip chart outside.

"Darn," she mumbled. She tried to move forward, but couldn't as she was tied to the flip chart which hung outside like a carnival poster. The more she struggled, the more the bungee cord pulled taut, the more the flip chart flapped and the door creaked.

"What in heaven's name?" exclaimed Miss Ogelvie, who'd scuttled her way to Millicent. "Who is this?" she asked, sliding her glasses down her nose.

Feeling somewhat absurd, Millicent said, "It's me, Millicent Madding. I'm kind of stuck, Miss Ogelvie."

"Evidently," said Miss Ogelvie. "Worse, you're being awfully disruptive. A library is a sacred place for study and the absorption of knowledge, Miss Madding. Quietness is paramount here. You, of all people, should know this, being a direct descendant of one of Masonville's finest librarians." Catching sight of the secret meeting room key around Millicent's neck, she added in a low voice, "Those of us who've been entrusted with access to the secret room must be especially respectful of the tenets of this institution, wouldn't you agree?"

Hardly in the mood or position for a lecture, much less

a long-winded one, Millicent said, "Yes, Miss Ogelvie. I wholeheartedly agree. But could you please help me?"

Miss Ogelvie smirked and gave the door a push. Millicent fell backward and, like a turtle flipped onto its back, floundered while Miss Ogelvie watched.

"Miss Ogelvie?" asked Millicent, panting.

"Oh, sorry," said Miss Ogelvie, helping Millicent up to a standing position with scarcely a grunt. "Why didn't you just undo the bungee cord?" Miss Ogelvie added, snapping the elastic band around Millicent's waist with her fingers.

Millicent didn't answer. For some inexplicable reason, she couldn't.

"You know," continued Miss Ogelvie, still whispering, "for such a smart young lady, you do some pretty nonsensical things. If I were you, I'd exchange an ounce of smarts for a quart of common sense. You won't get yourself stuck in doors with common sense."

Millicent knew that, by and large, adults dispensed advice every chance they got. Sometimes, the advice was useful, sometimes not. However, Millicent thought Miss Ogelvie's advice was downright rude.

"Miss Ogelvie—" Millicent started. She intended to tell her off, to tell her how much common sense she had at her beck and call. But she didn't. Miss Ogelvie cut a scary silhouette. Instead, Millicent walked on. "Thank you," she called to Miss Ogelvie, who looked at her in bewilderment.

Millicent dodged into the first aisle of the fiction section. She peered around the end cap. No bullies. She snuck two more aisles over and positioned herself between the bookcases, her flip chart knocking a book off a shelf in the process. *Oops*, she thought, carefully replacing the book. The sound of the book falling didn't attract any attention, so she moved forward to the nonfiction section.

Behind the last nonfiction bookshelf, she paused. She heard voices.

"Give that back," a girl's voice said in a stern tone.

Tonisha, thought Millicent.

"And what are you gonna do if I don't give it back?" Nina's deep and ugly voice replied. "Rhyme me till I choke? Yeah, right. Death by poetry."

Fletch and Pollywog laughed uproariously.

Millicent parted some biographies and peeked between them. Tonisha and the bullies stood a few yards from the children's book room. The secret meeting room entrance was just a little farther away.

Nina stood nose to nose with Tonisha, while Fletch and Pollywog looked on. Nina held Tonisha's precious note-book—the one in which Tonisha wrote all her poetry—at arm's length behind her. Given Nina's unnaturally long limb, the notebook hovered well out of Tonisha's reach.

"I wanna see what's in it," said Pollywog, hopping up and down, trying to snatch the book from Nina's grasp.

"You wouldn't get it," Tonisha said under her breath. "It's not a picture book." A bead of perspiration trickled down her forehead.

"I've always wondered why you and your weirdo friends

always go to the library," Nina said to Tonisha. "I think we'll wait here until they all show up."

Tonisha gritted her teeth.

"While we're waiting, I'll read us all a dumb poem. Let me see, here," said Nina, pushing Tonisha away with her right hand while flicking the notebook open with her left.

"Aw, c'mon," said Fletch. "Don't we got better things to do?"

Have, thought Millicent. *Don't we* have *better things to do?*

"Shut up," said Nina.

I've got to help Tonisha, thought Millicent. *But how?*

Laid out in a horseshoe arrangement of seven bookshelves, the nonfiction section opened up to the French doors that separated the children's room from the rest of the library. With a little care, Millicent could skirt the nonfiction area's perimeter and wind up at the tip of the horseshoe. What she'd do when she got there was a mystery, but she hoped to devise a scheme on the way.

She got down on all fours and started crawling so as not to be seen.

Meanwhile, Nina located a poem and started reading it. "'My Prince Charming,'" she read, "'in his castle bright, will one day set my wrong heart right.'"

"That's personal. Give it," said Tonisha, trying to grab the book.

"This is lame," said Nina, blocking Tonisha with her right arm. "Who is it about?"

"No one," said Tonisha, looking down.

"A personal poem about a fake prince?" asked Nina. Tonisha looked away. Nina made a crusty expression, dropping her jaw into an ugly gape. "How pathetic," she added in her grating voice.

"I think it's kinda nice," said Fletch.

"What?" asked Nina, glaring over her shoulder at Fletch.

"In a geeky kinda way," Fletch mumbled in return.

Millicent reached the last bookcase and stopped. She had an idea. She unstrapped the easel and the flip chart and took off her backpack and unzipped it.

Though it was still in development, she'd been toying with an invention she thought could get Tonisha out of her present pickle. Millicent had begun working on it while she had laryngitis earlier that year. Determined never again to be voiceless, she devised the VocoPad. The VocoPad was a miniature keyboard and looked as unimpressive as a regular computer keyboard. However, the VocoPad could do something a normal keyboard couldn't: it could record and store the nuances of your voice through a tiny microphone; then, as the need arose, speak what you typed on it, sounding just like you.

Millicent found the VocoPad and deprogrammed it, erasing all traces of her voice. Then she aimed the invention at Nina and waited for her to talk. She didn't have to wait long.

"I'm making up my own poem," Nina announced,

chuckling and waving Tonisha's notebook over her head. "Roses are red, violets are blue . . ."

Tonisha bit her lower lip.

"This book's gonna be torched by you know who," Nina said triumphantly. "Fletch. You got any matches?" she added, extending her palm.

Fletch dug through his pockets.

"No!" Tonisha yelped.

Fletch hesitated, then continued searching his pockets.

Millicent had never typed so fast in her life. Her fingers flew across the VocoPad's keyboard. She turned up the volume as high as it would go and pushed the enter key. Nothing happened. Millicent jiggled the VocoPad. Nothing. Millicent punched the enter key again. Suddenly, Nina's voice filled the entire library from the rotunda to the children's section.

"WE AIN'T AFRAID OF NO STINKIN' MISS OGELVIE!"

The exclamation was so loud, Millicent gasped and dropped the VocoPad.

Equally shocked at hearing the sound of her own voice coming from every which way, Nina dropped Tonisha's book of poetry. "What the—?" she asked.

Seizing the opportunity, Tonisha bent down and grabbed her notebook. Like a quarterback, she clutched the book close to her chest, weaving from side to side, as if one of the bullies would tackle her. Her headwrap wagged like a scolding finger.

Leaving the VocoPad where it had fallen, Millicent

typed another sentence on it. Shortly, Nina's voice rever-berated throughout the library.

"RIGHT, FLETCH? RIGHT, POLLYWOG?" Nina's mechanical impersonator screamed. "BRING IT ON, LIBRARY WOMAN!"

Nina twirled around, her eyes darting. Fletch looked around, too. Pollywog said, "Hey, Nina. Cool trick. I didn't know you were a ventila—ventrila . . . I didn't know you could throw your voice."

"I can't, you idiot," said Nina.

Thunderous footsteps echoed in the bookcase canyons, approaching with the speed of a charging bison.

"Uh-oh," whispered Nina.

Tonisha happened to glance in Millicent's direction, a glimmer of relief washing across her face. "Run," Millicent mouthed. But rather than running toward the children's sec-tion, Tonisha dashed for the bookcase where Millicent was hiding and collapsed behind it—and not a moment too soon.

"Did you do that?" whispered Tonisha.

"Shhh," warned Millicent.

Miss Ogelvie exploded into the clearing, practically snort-ing steam from her broad and slightly hairy nostrils. Planting her feet a yard apart, she jammed her fists into her hips.

"The sanctity of my library," she growled, "has been dis-turbed."

"What is—" said Pollywog softly.

"Sanctity," said Miss Ogelvie knowingly, "is the sacred condition of silence that my library normally enjoys."

Pollywog shrugged.

"Out," said Miss Ogelvie, pointing to the front door.

"Hey—" said Fletch.

"Out," said Miss Ogelvie, flexing her Shakespeare-tattooed bicep.

Fletch and Pollywog looked to Nina for a cue. Nina stared at Shakespeare's bulging face.

"C'mon," Nina said. "We'll get Fontaine," she added, scowling toward Tonisha and Millicent, "and Madding and the rest of 'em later. They're gonna pay."

As the trio shuffled away with Miss Ogelvie at their heels, Millicent heaved a sigh. Since the VocoPad worked—even if only after a shake and repeated attempts—then the chances of her new invention working were pretty good. She grinned to herself and collected her things.

"Thanks, Millicent," Tonisha said.

Millicent unlocked the secret chamber with the key she wore around her neck on a silk ribbon.

There were two keys to the secret chamber. The original belonged to Millicent. The second was a copy, cut because Roderick demanded it. He had complained that Millicent was always late and that the Wunderkinder couldn't dilly-dally, waiting around for her. She reluctantly complied and had a duplicate made, which Roderick wore around his neck on a chain.

To this day, it bothered Millicent that Roderick wore a Madding heirloom around his chubby, pink neck.

Millicent descended the stone stairs that lead to the

chamber, Tonisha close behind.

Tonisha tugged on Millicent's sleeve. "I owe you," she said.

"I'll be collecting shortly," Millicent said.

"What do you mean, you'll be collecting?" asked Tonisha in a hushed voice.

"You'll see," said Millicent.

"No," Tonisha said, grabbing Millicent's arm. "Tell me now. I don't like surprises."

Millicent set her things down. "If I tell you, you have to promise you'll stick up for me. No matter what."

"I promise."

"On a stack of your poems?"

"On a stack of my poems."

"I'm launching a new invention today," Millicent whispered.

"Oh, no," Tonisha grumbled. She plopped herself down on a stone step and started mumbling to herself. "Girl, I can't believe you got yourself into this. You should have seen this coming, like it had flashing lights on it and a siren going wheee-ah-wheee-ah-wheee. . . ." She waved her hands imitating a siren's lights.

"Tonisha, that's not nice," Millicent said, sitting next to her.

"Let me tell you about not nice. Not nice is that thing you made to do my wraps. What was it called? The Twist-O-Luxe Headwrap Wrapper?" Tonisha hissed. "Nearly strangled me senseless."

Millicent clicked her tongue. "I already apologized for that. Besides, this is different. I think I've hit on something that'll change our lives."

"My life does not need changing, Millicent," Tonisha said. "It's fine the way it is."

"Oh, is it?"

"It is."

"And you enjoy having moments like that in your life," Millicent said, pointing her thumb up the stairs. "The daily taunting and teasing. You like those moments."

"No," Tonisha said reluctantly.

"So your life does need changing," Millicent said, feeling victorious. "What would you say if I told you my invention will get those bullies to stop tormenting us? What would you say if I told you that it will render them harmless?" She stood. "What would you say if I told you that, with my newest invention, the worst you'll ever see from them is a dopey grin?"

A spark lit in Tonisha's eyes. "It'll do that?"

Millicent discreetly crossed her fingers. "It will."

"I did promise to stick up for you."

"You did."

Tonisha clutched her poetry notebook to her chest, deep in thought. "Girl," she finally said, rising, "we've got a product to launch."

Four

The Wunderkind Club was already in session when Millicent and Tonisha finally tumbled into the secret chamber.

A long, antique wooden table sat in the center of the windowless room. On the table squatted a tarnished silver candelabrum supporting thirty burning candles. Millicent's great-great-great-great grandmother had left it there, along with the acres of well-preserved books lining the walls.

Roderick sat at his usual place, the head of the table, twisting his red bow tie. Pollock Wong, the Wunderkind artist, sat to Roderick's right, his glossy black hair reflecting the candlelight, except in those areas where it was splattered with paint. Next to Pollock, Leon Finklebaum snored quietly, his head cast over the back of his chair. Juanita Romero Alonso, the Wunderkind musician, was talking.

Millicent slipped into a chair off to the side, setting her presentation materials down with a thud. Everyone except Leon turned to look at Millicent and Tonisha.

Tonisha pulled up a chair and sat at the table. Since she was club secretary, her place at the table was reserved.

"Look what twosome decided to join us," said Roderick. Tonisha smirked at him.

"We've already started, but we can backtrack," Roderick stated flatly. "Juanita, please repeat what you just told those of us who were on time to this meeting." He nodded to Juanita, who sat to his left.

"Um, okay," Juanita said, petting her violin case. "As you all know, Masonville's annual Young Talent Extravaganza is less than a week away. I'm proud to say that I've perfected the Prokofiev piece I've been practicing in time for the competition. I'm giving a preview of it at the student assembly at school." She stood and curtsied.

"Very good," Roderick approved. "Tonisha, you should have notes on Juanita's rehearsal in your minutes from the last meeting. Could you read those? Provided you're ready."

"I am, I am," Tonisha said, fumbling with her notebook. She flipped some pages, stood, and smacked her lips in preparation.

Whenever Tonisha read, she'd sway from side to side,

which made whoever was listening sway from side to side, too. As she leaned, it looked as if the headwrap she was wearing that day would come toppling down. The Wunderkinder couldn't help but hope it would stay intact.

Tonisha read from her notepad, swaying, candlelight and shadows writing sonnets across her face:

"Juanita Romero Alonso,
Having gone completely gonzo,
Fiddled her little socks off
In a tribute to Rachmaninoff—"

"Fiddle," interrupted Juanita, "is such a rustic term." She caressed her violin case. "This is a VI-O-LIN."

"Too many syllables," Tonisha said.

"And it wasn't Rachmaninoff. That was the meeting before," Juanita said.

"Right," Tonisha said. "And 'fiddled her little socks off in a tribute to Prokofiev' sounds so much better."

Juanita grimaced.

Millicent squirmed in her seat. Tonisha's minutes never sounded like real minutes. Millicent preferred it when Leon was secretary. At least his minutes were shorter since he slept most of the time.

Tonisha went on:

"Juanita Romero Alonso
Fiddled her song on and on so

Roderick begged her to stop it,
Then he took the floor just to top it."

She finished the poem dramatically with a sigh loud enough to wake Leon and a bow so low everyone shouted, "Whoa," as her headwrap came dangerously close to falling off and into the candelabrum. She snapped her body upright, and the headwrap boinged back into place.

"In other words," said Roderick, blinking, "last month Juanita worked on a new violin piece."

"Plainly put," said Tonisha as she sat.

"Mmm," mumbled Leon, reclining in his chair and closing his eyes.

"Who would like to go next?" Roderick asked. Millicent raised her hand. "Everett, you have the floor," Roderick said.

"It's not Everett anymore. I've told you that. I go by Pollock now," Pollock huffed. "I've renamed myself after Jackson Pollock the—"

"Abstract expressionist painter, I know," Roderick said.

Pollock folded his arms over his paint-splattered shirt. "I'm also entered in Masonville's Young Talent Extravaganza. I'll be exhibiting a few paintings at the opening day student assembly, too."

"Well done, Ever— Pollock," Roderick said. Millicent raised her hand, but Roderick leaned forward to address Leon, the math-whiz Wunderkind. "Leon? We haven't heard from you yet."

Leon snored louder.

"Leon?" Roderick asked. "LEON!"

"Four thousand three hundred and ninety-six!" Leon blurted, suddenly awake.

"Dreaming about numbers again," Pollock mumbled. "Go back to sleep, Leon."

"All righty," Leon said, then put his head down on the table.

"Tonisha, weren't you working on a little poem for the extravaganza?" Roderick asked.

Tonisha arched an eyebrow in his direction. "I'm still working on my epic poem."

"Is that it for old business?" Roderick asked Tonisha, his eyes rolling.

"Verily," she replied.

"Good," Roderick said, "now, who wants to be first to share their most recent accomplishments?" Millicent raised her hand, but Roderick's own arm shot up as if he had no control over it. "Looks like I'm first."

The Wunderkinder groaned and everyone leaned back in their chairs, readying themselves to listen to Roderick.

"You all know," he began, "but it bears repeating that my parents are both highly successful in their chosen fields. My father as senior partner in Biggleton, Wigglebum, and Higglebee, attorneys-at-law and my mother as—"

"President and CEO of Beauty Goo Cosmetics," the Wunderkinder said in unison, as if they were singing a hymn.

"Yes," said Roderick, sneering at them. "Despite your impolite interruption—which I take as anticipation—I will begin at the beginning and leave no stone unturned as I recount the fascinating month I had. It will undoubtedly inspire you to lift your dreary lives to a higher level of aspiration. You, too, can be like me."

The Wunderkinder balked, whispering to each other things like "The nerve."

A year ago, they'd asked Roderick to join the Wunderkind Club because he'd been teased at school for being smart, but also because he seemed to have a knack for running things efficiently. Little did they know then that his organizational skills relied on a heavy dose of bossiness.

Roderick went on for nearly fifteen minutes, talking about how he helped his father prepare a legal case for which he couldn't share the details—attorney-client privilege, you know—and about how he went with his mother to a cosmetics convention in Pinnimuk City where he, personally, met the president of So Much Stuff, So Little Time department stores.

He was nearing the end of his speech. Leon was snoring. Pollock was doodling on a scrap of paper. Juanita was humming to herself, her hand inching toward her violin. Tonisha was writing and Millicent was feeling antsy. She wanted so badly to give her presentation, her sluggishness of that morning now a memory.

"And that, my fellow Wunderkinder," said Roderick, "was what I did last month." The Wunderkinder applauded halfheartedly. "Is there other new business?" Millicent raised her hand.

"Millicent, you have the floor," Roderick said.

Millicent bounded to the head of the table, her presentation materials in hand. She wrestled with the three-legged easel until it was properly set up, slapped her flip chart onto it, then turned back the first sheet of paper. She whipped out a felt-tip pen from her waistband and spun around to face the group. Her foot snagged on the easel. It leaned and she frantically grappled with it, but it crashed to the floor.

"Eighty-seven thousand five hundred and six!" Leon yelled, his eyes wide open.

"Buzzing Millicent," said Tonisha, scribbling in her tablet. "Caught in the web of her spider easel, a fly bearing products with which to . . . tease-l." She scratched out the last part.

"Wow," said Pollock Wong, putting his hands behind his head and his feet on the table. "Somebody's anxious."

Roderick nodded.

Millicent repositioned her easel and took a deep breath. Whatever pitch she had rehearsed escaped her. She felt daring. She felt hyped. She decided to wing it.

She wasn't as good an artist as Pollock but she drew on the flip chart anyway. She started by sketching a pudgy figure in a striped shirt with a baseball cap on its round head; next, a tall figure as thin as a tetherball pole; and, finally, an apelike creature with long hair, wearing a halter top, whose overlarge knuckles scraped the horizon line of the picture. Her memory still fresh from her encounter with them, Millicent thought she did a decent job of capturing the bullies' likenesses.

"Wunderkinder," she said, stepping away from the flip chart. "Do you know who these people are?"

They leaned forward, quiet. She had their attention.

"Well, the quality of your drawing is rather primitive," said Pollock Wong, "and the proportions are a bit questionable, but I'd say the chubby one looks like Pollywog Jones, the thin one looks like Fletch Farnsworth, and the chimp bears an uncanny resemblance to Nina 'The Knuckle' Kwaikowski."

"Exactly, on all accounts," said Millicent, wagging her felt-tip pen at him.

"Not bad," Leon said to Pollock. "I thought the chimp was Mrs. Bleeker."

"Mrs. Bleeker does kind of look like a chimp, doesn't she?" asked Juanita.

"A chimp," said Tonisha, her face buried in her notepad, "or a rhesus monkey."

"Need I remind you all—especially you, Leon—that regardless of what primate she resembles, Mrs. Bleeker doesn't wear halter tops?" Pollock asked.

"Oh. I thought it was a lobster bib," said Leon. Everyone smirked at him. "Hey," he whined, "I saw her at Captain Dandy's Seafood Shanty on my birthday. She was wearing one then."

"Go back to sleep, Leon," said Pollock. "The caricature is clearly of Nina Kwaikowski."

"Nina Kwaikowski," said Tonisha, still writing in her notepad. "Now there's a rhesus monkey if I've ever seen one."

"You're all getting off track," Millicent said, huffing. She was losing their attention. Uncle Phineas said losing an audience's attention spelled trouble.

"Continue," Roderick advised.

"School starts on Monday," she said, collecting herself, "and these animals will be roaming the halls again." She pointed at the flip chart with her pen. "They will be waiting for us with kick-me signs." She began pacing, slowly, deliberately, making eye contact with each Wunderkind. They'd all been picked on by bullies, she reminded them. "They will pick their noses and, with their boogery fingers poised, flick nasal nuggets at us."

Tonisha stopped writing and looked up from her notepad. "Vividly disgusting," she said.

Millicent ignored her. Instead, she strolled behind Roderick, bent down, and hissed in his ear, "Why, just this morning, on my way to this very meeting—I was confronted by Fletch, Pollywog, and Nina." She straightened up and added, "So was Tonisha."

The Wunderkinder turned to look at Tonisha, who'd stopped writing.

Suddenly, the air was pierced with a screechy, horror-movie tune—*eeek, eeek, eeek, eeek.*

"Juanita—" Millicent growled. Juanita put her bow and violin down.

Millicent went into grim detail as she recounted her run-in with the bullies. Her vivid description of Nina's foot on her car had them spellbound. Then she went into the incident with Tonisha, lingering on every aspect for dramatic effect. When she finished, the brick room was as silent as a tomb.

Juanita petted her violin. Pollywog Jones had kidnapped it once and had placed a ransom note in her locker demanding she do his homework for a whole week in exchange for it. Pollock scowled. Nina "the Knuckle" Kwaikowski had once punched a clay sculpture he'd prepared for a city-wide youth art show.

"So?" asked Roderick, his voice echoing. "What's so new about that?" Millicent could tell by his shaky tone that Roderick was trying to appear cool and unmoved. He, of all the Wunderkinder, was most acquainted with the bullies' ways, having once been pushed into the Winifred T. Langley Memorial Fountain by all three of them.

Millicent squinted at Roderick, inhaled deeply, then turned her attention to the other Wunderkinder. "I have invented a new product to keep bullies away: Bully-Be-Gone."

At this point it was hard for Millicent to know who to listen to because they all began jabbering at the same time.

"Oh, no."

"I can't believe this—"

"Not me—"

"You try it."

"No way."

"Never again."

Millicent raised her voice above the others'. "Excuse me," she said.

They chattered on. Except Tonisha, who watched quietly.

"Excuse me," she yelled, then lowered her voice because they were, after all, in a library. "Need I remind you that—despite the excess saliva it produced—you thrilled at my Ever-Juicy Gum Enhancer pellet? You were awestruck at the effectiveness of the I've-Got-Rhythm Boogie Belt—which reminds me, Leon, I still owe you a refund for that unfortunate punch table incident at the spring dance. And, though I've yet to work out the kinks in the flavored ink and paper, you were all duly impressed with Fax-A-Snack." She stopped and stared them down. "This invention is my most potent of all."

Tonisha forced a smile. The remaining Wunderkinder were quiet, their eyes ablaze with distrust—an ominous effect further enhanced by the dancing candlelight.

Five

After Millicent left for the Wunderkind meeting, Uncle Phineas tidied the kitchen, with the help of the Robotic Chef, who'd started scraping the leftovers into Madame Curie's food dish. The Robotic Chef missed the dish completely, dumping the meager leftovers on the floor.

"Dish? Floor? Yes. Makes no difference to you, does it?" Uncle Phineas asked the cat, who'd already gobbled her meal. "You made quick work of that. And I must make quick work of repairing these trousers."

He turned around to show the cat the deflated chair hanging off his pants. Madame Curie batted at it as if it were a toy. Uncle Phineas laughed and then went upstairs to his bedroom to change, the cat following him, dodging and attacking his chair pants.

Uncle Phineas changed, shaved, and applied his favorite cologne. He sprayed a cloud of it, walked through the mist, then spritzed some under his armpits and behind his ears. Named Strong Like Bull, the cologne claimed to make one man smell like ten men. He had bought ten cases of Strong Like Bull many years ago when he'd heard the manufacturer would be discontinuing it. His stash of the fragrance had soured over time, yet even now he wore it because it had been his wife's favorite scent. "My big, strong inventor," she used to say to him, so close her breath fogged his glasses.

"Just for you, my dear," he said to a photo of Aunt Felicity he kept in the bathroom. "Wherever you are." He kissed his fingertip and pressed it against her picture on her helmet.

Millicent's aunt Felicity had been a human cannonball for the Sprightly Sisters All-Woman Circus. She called herself an airborne artillery artist. All the photos of her showed her standing next to a cannon, in a polka-dotted leotard and satin cape and coordinating striped helmet.

One ill-fated day, during a matinee performance, she was catapulted through the top of the circus tent. Uncle Phineas was there. Long after the audience had gone, he sat stunned, looking at the hole through which she'd exited. He wished he had the power to rewind the matinee. If he had the power, he'd once told Millicent, he would make the elephants go backward, make the lady clowns stuff themselves back into their wonky-wheeled car. In his fantasy scenario, Aunt Felicity would return through the tent roof, closing the hole behind her as if it were zippered.

However, Aunt Felicity was never seen again.

"Wherever you are, my dear." Uncle Phineas sighed. He turned and headed downstairs, the cat trailing him, still fascinated by the deflated chair pants he had tucked under his arm. He entered the lab and laid the pants on a table. The cat leaped onto the table and pawed at the pants. Something beneath them caught her attention. She began toying with that instead.

"Madame Curie," Uncle Phineas said, "you are being a pest today. I cannot work with you here. Perhaps you'd enjoy a romp outside." As he picked her up, she took one last swipe at her new plaything. "What is this?" Uncle Phineas asked, examining the aluminum packet with which the cat had been so taken. He set the cat down on the floor. "'Bully-Be-Gone. Free sample. Repels bullies, thugs, and other unsavory characters. Body heat activated,'" he read from the label. He smiled. "Now, isn't that noble? Yes? Well, one never knows when one might have a run-in with a bully." He tore the packet open, brought it to his nose, sniffed the contents. "Odd. No smell." He smeared the packet behind his ears and under his arms.

He lifted the cat off the floor, brought her outside through the lab door, and set her down on the lawn. He stretched out his arms as if embracing the entire neighborhood.

"What a grand day, Madame Curie," he said. "The air is filled with magic."

The air was indeed filled with something he couldn't see.

Unbeknownst to Uncle Phineas, the Bully-Be-Gone intermingled with the Strong Like Bull cologne. The chemicals in each were both attracted to, yet also repelled by, one another. He'd become a sort of living firecracker. The combination of his fermented cologne and Millicent's invention, set off by his body temperature, was phenomenal. Like a Roman fountain, he was literally shooting tiny sparks of Strong Like Bull and Bully-Be-Gone.

Ping! Ping! Ping! The molecules shot hundreds of feet into the air where they were lifted by the breeze.

Over the next few days, they were carried past great stretches of farmland, over forests, and beyond hills to Pinnimuk City. There they were swirled in circular currents by passing cars, propelled by steam rising from vents in the sidewalks, jetted through the air again by the breeze.

They wafted through Pinnimuk City Central Park, between the trees, past the playground, over the lake.

When the invisible droplets finally landed, they came to rest on a homeless lady lying on a grassy knoll, a rock as her pillow, under layers and layers of newspapers. She opened one eye, then the other. She inhaled the wonderful scent that rained on her cheeks and forehead and nose.

What was it? It smelled, to her, like a good many things at once. With her head tilted back, she mentally listed the smells: popcorn, elephants, and gunpowder.

There was a fourth smell she couldn't place. She squinted, trying to recall what it was. She thought if love had an aroma, it might smell like this; tender and courageous. She thought harder. It wasn't one but two distinct bouquets: a dashing young inventor and a cologne called Strong Like Bull. Six smells in all—the sum of her former life, fragrant as a posy.

She looked at the sky and sat up, gathering the sheets of newspaper around her as if they were the children she'd never had. A single tear rolled down her cheek, paving a streak of fresh skin through the soil on her face. Then she clutched both hands over her heart. She remembered who she was.

Six

Millicent studied the gathering of Wunderkinder in the secret room. From Pollock's glower to Roderick's sour expression, each face doubted her. Except Tonisha's. She seemed to be waiting for a cue.

"Tonisha," Millicent said, "this is where you come in."

She shot out of her chair. "Millicent rescued me from Nina with one of her inventions," she announced. "I fully endorse her current endeavor." She sat back down.

"Thank you," Millicent said, winking at Tonisha. "With that proof statement . . ." She produced a bottle of the blue substance from her backpack. "I present to you, Bully-Be-

Gone: soon to be available in cologne for men, perfume for women, and also in a handy, pocket-sized deodorant. For you outdoorsy types, I'll have Bully-Be-Gone Cream with UV protection."

Millicent set her collection of bottles on the table.

Roderick clicked his tongue. "Your inventions don't work. Something always goes wrong," he said. "No offense, Millicent."

She didn't believe Roderick. He *did* mean to offend her.

"There may have been a few mishaps along the way," Millicent said.

"Yeah," said Pollock, pointing his finger at Millicent. "I'll never forget your Nail Clipper Mittens."

"But your nails did look spiffy," Tonisha said, "once you looked past the bandages."

"There have been more than a few mishaps," Juanita said, not playing her violin this time.

"But that is why I am offering free samples of Bully-Be-Gone," Millicent continued. She reached into her backpack, retrieving a handful of foil packets that she dealt to the Wunderkinder as one might playing cards. "Try it for a week. If you're not completely satisfied, you've lost nothing. On the other hand, if you're pleased with the results, you'll receive a twenty percent discount on your first purchase of Bully-Be-Gone."

Millicent had given this part plenty of thought. Giving freebies was known as promotion. Uncle Phineas had told her freebies, like shampoo samples that came in the mail or taste tests of chili con carne at the grocery store, were among the best ways to get people to return for more of your product. And, he'd said, people love getting something for nothing—they couldn't possibly reject free samples. He was right. The Wunderkinder took the packets, some cautiously, others eagerly, as if they'd been handed complimentary fries with the purchase of a burger.

Millicent felt pretty pleased with herself.

"Well, hey," said Leon, examining his sample, "I'll try anything if it's free."

"Why not?" asked Pollock. "At least it doesn't have moving parts."

"I'll give it a shot," said Juanita.

Roderick was the only Wunderkind not wholly convinced. "And just how does this Bully whatever supposedly work?" he asked, leaning back in his chair.

Millicent turned the page on her flip chart and drew a nose on the left side of the page and a brain on the right side. "The olfactory organ," she said, pointing to the nose, "is the most direct connection to the brain." She drew a line between the two. "Research shows that scent is the most powerful trigger to memory."

"Scent memory," Roderick said. "Smells make you remember things. We know."

Millicent scowled. "Yes, but the nose isn't very selective, is it? It smells what it smells by chance, and there's no guarantee what the brain will remember because of the smell. Pleasant memories? Unpleasant memories? Who knows?"

"Are you getting around to making a point?" Roderick asked.

"Bully-Be-Gone induces only pleasant scent memories," Millicent said triumphantly. "Only the loveliest, happiest, dreamiest moments in a person's life."

"The smell of lavender always reminds me of my granny," Tonisha said wistfully.

"So what?" Roderick asked in a terse voice, the veins on his neck bulging. "I don't see how that'll keep Pollywog from taking Juanita's violin hostage again or Nina from destroying Pollock's artwork." He added quietly, "Or all three of them from pushing me into the fountain."

"Think about it, Roderick," Millicent said. "It will only affect a person with a bad attitude. For the person who's in good spirits, a pleasant memory would mean nothing. It would simply be absorbed into his or her generally cheery attitude, kind of like a drop of cream in a butter churn. But for the person who is perpetually cranky, well, a pleasant memory would turn him or her into a big pile of sentimental mush." She circled the table, closing in on Roderick. "Now, whom do you know who's perpetually cranky?"

"Principal Pennystacker," Leon said. "He's a grouch."

"Other than Principal Pennystacker," Millicent said.

"Nina, Fletch, and Pollywog," Tonisha stated.

"That's right," Millicent said. "And, by using Bully-Be-Gone, you'll soon see those three nasty rats turn into three schmaltzy mice."

"Indeed," Roderick said, placing the packet in his chest

pocket, behind his pocket protector. "What harm could come of using this?"

Millicent looked at him quizzically, tilting her head. She wished she could stand on her head at that moment. She was sure Roderick Biggleton the Third would seem less grumpy when viewed upside down.

Seven

The homeless woman patted and shook the pockets of her overcoat for change. She worked her way up, down, and around to the other pockets in her various articles of clothing: two cardigans, a vest, three pairs of pants, and a skirt. Not a clink or clack. Nothing. She turned her pockets inside out, just to be certain there wasn't a lonely penny or stray nickel. She'd need money in order to make the trip home.

"Home," she said to herself. She remembered home was in Masonville in an old house with a porch and trees and a lawn and an inventor. "Home. No place like it—can't live with it, can't live without it; a penny saved is a penny earned for bus fare." She cawed at her joke.

Her lack of funds didn't bother her. Nothing could destroy her perky mood now that her memory had returned. She'd figure out a way to get some money. She had managed for the twenty years she'd lived on the streets, she'd manage now, too.

She spent the entire day walking around the park and looking for money. She tried shaking a few parking meters for loose quarters and scrounging under park benches for change that might have fallen out of people's pockets. Her efforts turned up a nickel, a paper clip, and a stick of gum still in its wrapper. That night, she went back to her rock and fell asleep, her good cheer intact because she knew, somehow, she'd get enough money for the bus ride home.

She awoke the next morning, chuckling to herself. She'd dreamed the lawn beneath her had turned into dollar bills.

A businessman sitting on a nearby park bench didn't seem to find her laughter amusing and shot her a nervous glare from behind his newspaper.

"That's some how do you do," she said, loud enough for the man to hear. "It just so happens you are in the presence of the Fabulous Flying Felicity—airborne artillery artist." She stood and curtsied, the ragged hem of her overcoat skimming the neatly trimmed lawn.

He tried to ignore her, snapping the paper, drawing it closer to his face.

"I came from up there," Felicity said, pointing to the sky, "but home is where I need to go now. Home to my inventor." She appraoched the man and peered over the top of his newspaper. "How much are bus trips to Masonville these days?"

The man appeared annoyed. "I don't know," he finally said. "I drive."

"Drive what?" she asked. She wasn't really interested in what he drove; she was making friendly conversation.

"A Humdinger Deluxa LX7-CWVi with a moonroof, leather seats, sixteen-speaker music system, two phones, a television, a hot tub, and a compact microwave oven," he said, crossing his legs assuredly.

This was the most the man had said to her thus far. She thought this odd. He hadn't introduced himself, but he had his transportation. Surely, he drove something grander than a plain old car. Also, it had to be pretty big with all those gizmos. "You drive a motor home every day?" she asked in disbelief, pulling her knit cap over her ears.

"Don't be absurd," the man scoffed. "If you must know, a Humdinger Deluxa is the luxury car of choice here in Pinnimuk City. Haven't you seen the billboards: 'That's a Humdinger of a Car'?"

"Well, la-di-dah," she said, swiveling her hips. She hadn't noticed the billboards. If the man had any sense, which apparently he didn't, he'd be aware that folks who are down on their luck rarely look up. Especially at advertisements for utterly extravagant things they can't afford.

"I fly," she continued, extending her arms before her as if she were diving. "Or, I would if I had my cannon, but I don't. So how's about some spare change? some excess coinage? some moolah? some dough? some—"

"All right," said the man impatiently. He tilted to one side, fiddled around in his pocket, handed her a five dollar bill, and frowned. "For heaven's sake, here. Now go away." He shooed her with his hand, a diamond ring on his finger glinting in the sun.

"Whoa," she exclaimed, holding the crinkled bill to the sun. Five whole dollars was more money than she'd hoped for and more than she'd seen for a very long time. "Jackpot! Round-trip fare, eh? Bad news—I'm not coming back."

"If we're both lucky," the man said under his breath.

"We are," Felicity said. "And thank you kindly. Gifts may not always be given kindly, but kindly they should be received." She spun a balletic spin, her coat tenting in a cloud of dust, and sauntered down the cement path toward Pinnimuk City Station, whistling a tune she made up as she went.

Eight

Winifred T. Langley Middle School, oddly enough, was named after the Bendable Francine Tippit.

In the early nineteen hundreds, Francine was the star of a traveling vaudeville show that went from city to city providing audiences with a variety of acts from comedy skits to song-and-dance routines. Francine's specialty in the lineup of acts was contortion. She could scrunch herself up so small she could fit into a paper grocery bag without tearing it. She could also sit on her own head while doing a handstand and play a toy piano with her toes.

Despite her fame and flexibility, Francine was a nervous

lady, prone to chewing her fingernails. Since she was a contortionist, she could also easily chew her toenails. Candid photographs from the period often showed her at social gatherings or backstage before a performance at Lulu Davinsky's Diamond Theater, arched backward, full circle, with her shoe off and her foot in her mouth.

One night, she was about to go onstage when she heard there was a big-time movie producer in the audience, scouting for his next star. Francine broke into a sweat. Having a movie producer in the audience meant she could either be discovered and become famous, or not and be stuck playing the vaudeville circuit for the rest of her days. Both possibilities petrified her. She slipped off her lace-up boots, curled herself back, grabbed her ankles, and began chewing the toenails of both feet. She did it for so long she passed out. Her misfortune didn't end there. Because she blacked out with her mouth clamped firmly on both feet, she rolled onstage like a hoop or wheel, then promptly rolled into the orchestra pit, hitting her head on a tuba.

When she awoke in Masonville Memorial Hospital, she'd forgotten who she was—she had amnesia.

A friend of Francine's, a practical joker and comedian named Hobart the Comic, was visiting when she woke up. He'd brought her more flowers than she'd ever seen, which wasn't much of a feat considering she couldn't remember ever seeing flowers before. Somehow, Hobart managed to convince her that her name was Winifred T. Langley and that she was among the most scholarly minds of her generation, able to speak seven languages and cook gourmet meals—neither of which she could do.

Winifred believed this jolly man with the armload of roses so totally that she went on to university, where she earned several foreign language degrees as well as a seat on the board of directors of Crusty Culinary College, a school for cooks of the highest order.

No one could have foretold her change in character. As a linguist, historian, and chef, she was calmer and happier than she'd ever been as a contortionist. Not wanting to break her spell of contentment, friends and strangers alike hid the photographs of her performing career and took to calling her Winifred to her face and behind her back. In time, most forgot her past as a double-jointed entertainer. The city erected a school and named it in her honor. She married Hobart the Comic, who'd also led her to believe they were engaged, and her nails—both finger and toe—grew back to admirable, polishable lengths.

By way of this series of freakish events, she became Masonville's first and only double-jointed professor and chef with a namesake educational institution.

However, life, as it is sometimes apt to, delivered Winifred another unexpected turn.

Among Winifred's many successes was Bistro Langley, a French restaurant she'd opened downtown. One night, she was in the kitchen preparing her signature creation, duck *à l'orange brûlée*, crisping its sugary surface with a blow-torch. Her hands were greasy with olive oil and the blow-torch slipped from her grip, setting a cutting board on fire as it fell to the floor behind her. Automatically, she bent over backward to pick it up.

This was the first time Winifred had bent over backward in many years. Perhaps the familiarity of the pose or the blood rushing to her head made it all come back to her in an upside-down flash: her real name, her previous life as a performer, the vaudeville stage, her nail-biting habit. Flames sizzled across the kitchen counters, licking up the trails of butter, lard, and oil. Soon, the walls were ablaze in an orange heat, which spread to the main dining area. She ran screaming out of the burning restaurant and never returned.

The next day the headline in the *Masonville Gazette* read, BISTRO LANGLEY TOAST, PROPRIETOR MISSING. A search party was formed. They found Francine at sunset, by Fisherperson's Wharf, lying on the shore chewing her toenails.

Just as she had forgotten her performing career when she collided with the tuba, she had now forgotten the foreign languages she'd learned, the historical facts, and her hundreds of original recipes. She whittled her finger and toenails back down to pathetic nubs. She remained married to Hobart the Comic, but theirs was a distant relationship; she couldn't bring herself to trust him. And, by then, the city wasn't about to change the name of Winifred T. Langley Middle School to the Bendable Francine Tippit Middle School.

The city did make one compromise. It constructed an enormous bronze statue of Francine in the school's front fountain. At the base of the statue was a tuba, from which water spouted. The statue itself depicted her reading a book in a classic contortionist's pose, her forearms and chest on the floor with her body arched so that she was sitting on her own head, her feet planted firmly in front of her.

Nowadays, the fountain had lost most of its meaning, except to those who were up on Masonville history. For the crankier teachers and administrative staff, it served as a cautionary sculpture to remind students to study hard or they might end up sitting in unfavorable places. For the custodians, it was a distorted, creepy thing to clean. For the cheerleaders, it was a pose they could only hope to strike.

For Millicent, who was up on Masonville history, the fountain inspired her to believe anything was possible.

Millicent sat on the edge of the fountain before school, waiting for Tonisha. She spritzed a little more of the new Bully-Be-Gone perfume on her neck, wrists, and ankles. She'd already put some on earlier that morning, but on Wednesdays she had one class with Fletch and two with Pollywog Jones and Nina "the Knuckle" Kwaikowski. She'd need maximum protection.

School had been in session for two days and drastic measures were called for. As far as Millicent knew, none of the Wunderkinder had tried Bully-Be-Gone. If she couldn't get them to try it, she wouldn't make any sales and she'd have to discontinue the product. She gave herself an extra squirt behind her ears. She would prove to them that Bully-Be-Gone worked.

She stood, peering into the distance for Tonisha.

"Millicent," hissed two voices in unison.

Millicent jumped. "Pollock? Juanita?" she asked, catching her breath. "You startled me. I didn't hear you coming." She looked around. "Where are you?" she asked.

"Over here," whispered Pollock.

Millicent circled the fountain. They weren't to be found.

"Pssst. Over here," whispered Juanita.

They couldn't be—she looked in the fountain. Nope, they weren't there.

"Nice shoes," said Pollock.

She looked down. Near her feet was a slatted metal drainage cover. Pollock and Juanita huddled in the drain, peering at her from behind the cover.

"What are you doing in there?" she asked, checking over her shoulder to see if anyone was watching.

"What does it look like?" asked Juanita. "Hiding, you moron."

"From?" asked Millicent.

"Pollywog and Nina," said Pollock, exasperated, as if Millicent should have guessed. "Is the coast clear?"

She surveyed their surroundings. In the distance, at the side of the main building, Pollywog and Nina were locking their bikes to the bike rack. There were those new bikes again, looking as if they'd still have price tags on them.

Millicent would have to inspect them for Mega-Stupenda Mart stickers, but first there was the matter of her friends in the sewer. Millicent waited until Nina and Pollywog entered school before removing the drainage cover. Why would her friends be hiding from Pollywog and Nina? Hadn't they applied Bully-Be-Gone? Wasn't it effective? She bit her lip, expecting the worst.

First, a smallish portfolio came through the hole, then a violin case in a backpack. Next, Pollock and Juanita crawled out of the drain, festooned with leaves and bits of moldy, rotted stuff. They brushed themselves off.

"We have a problem with your invention," said Pollock, glaring at Millicent and swiping the last piece of crud from his paint-splattered shirt.

"Yeah," added Juanita, picking a crusty something or other out of her hair. "It's not doing its job."

"I don't understand," said Millicent.

"Pollywog has been following Juanita everywhere," said Pollock, "and I can't shake Nina. I go to my locker, she's there; I walk home, she's in my shadow."

"Have they threatened you guys? Harmed you? Tripped you, hit you, spit at you?" asked Millicent, trying to disguise the worry in her voice.

"No," answered Juanita.

"Nope," said Pollock.

"Then what's wrong?" Millicent asked.

"They're following us—that's what's wrong," said Juanita.

Millicent gave her a questioning stare.

"Yesterday," Juanita continued, "Pollywog asked Mr. Cleff if he could join the orchestra."

"So?" asked Millicent. "Maybe he's discovered a hidden talent for music."

"He can't even play the triangle," Juanita shot back. "Sat there throughout an entire concerto, staring at me, dinging in all the wrong places."

"And last night," said Pollock, "Nina called my house— left a message. She just wanted to chat. About *van Gogh*. Don't you think that's slightly off?" His arms were hinged shut across his chest, his head cocked to one side.

Millicent shrugged. "Sounds like a nice gesture," she said.

But she wasn't fooling herself. She did think it sounded slightly off—bizarre, in fact. A bully joining the orchestra? A bully phoning a Wunderkind just to chat about an artist? Strange. Still, she'd need more evidence to show if her invention was the cause of this unusual set of circumstances. Maybe there was another reason.

"Perhaps they're being pleasant for a change," suggested Millicent.

"Pleasant?" asked Pollock.

"Pleasant," said Juanita, "would be if they left us alone. Wasn't that the point of Bully-Be-Gone? To make them leave us alone?"

Millicent nodded.

"The back-to-school assembly is in five minutes,

Millicent," Pollock said, staring her down. "Ring any bells?"

Millicent thought about it. "Um, no," she said.

"Let me remind you," Pollock said. "As part of the student assembly and as a celebration of the best of Winifred T. Langley, Mr. Pennystacker asked me to exhibit my artwork."

"Uh-huh?" asked Millicent.

"He slated Juanita for a violin solo," said Pollock.

"Uh-huh?" asked Millicent, breaking into a sweat.

"Which means the whole school will be watching," said Pollock.

"Uh-huh?" asked Millicent, twisting the hem of her sweater.

"It had all better go smoothly," Pollock warned.

"There is something wrong here, Millicent," said Juanita, shaking her finger.

"And we strongly suggest— Oh, my gosh. There they are," whispered Pollock. "Run, Juanita."

Millicent turned to see Pollywog and Nina standing in the main entrance, grinning and waving. Pollock and Juanita bolted. Pollock's portfolio flapped at his side like a broken wing. Juanita's violin case bounced in her backpack. They headed toward the rear of the school with Pollywog and Nina chasing them.

Millicent watched, completely befuddled. None of it made any sense. Bully-Be-Gone was supposed to keep bullies at a distance. It was supposed to make bullies kinder and gentler by jogging their scent memories. It was not supposed to . . . draw them to you.

In seconds, Millicent caught sight of Tonisha's head-wrap about a block away, a glowing yellow-and-brown-spotted tower of fabric, like a headless giraffe lumbering down the street. Next to it, she saw Fletch Farnsworth's unmistakable blond hair. She gasped. What was Tonisha doing walking with Fletch? Was Tonisha in danger? As they rounded the corner of the school's hedge, she saw that Fletch was riding his glistening green bicycle. He wobbled in order to keep up with Tonisha's slower walking pace. Was he bullying her? Millicent squinted. It didn't look like he was being mean. In fact, the two of them were laughing. This was beyond strange; it was unnatural. A bully and a Wunderkind, walking to school together? Unheard of. She clutched her books to her chest.

It was becoming clear to her—though she tried to shake off the realization as one might a mosquito—Bully-Be-Gone was attracting bullies.

They came closer. Fletch said something to Tonisha, waved good-bye, and rode away to the bike racks. Tonisha waved, too, which wasn't nearly as disturbing as the kooky look on her face. Millicent ran to her.

"What was that all about?" she asked, panting.

"Are you aware Fletch writes music?" Tonisha asked.

Millicent frowned. "Huh?"

"Yeah, he writes music."

"And—?"

"And he serenaded me with a song he wrote especially for me."

"Oh, dear."

"He had trouble rhyming my name. The best he could do was, 'You smell like a freesia, my lovely Tonisha,'" said Tonisha. "Isn't that the nicest attempt at a ditty you've ever heard?"

"But he hates you," Millicent said. "He hates all of us Wunderkinder."

"Millicent, dear," Tonisha said, "that was not a hate song. Quite the contrary."

"Tonisha—"

"His eyes are hazel. And on his cheek he has an adorable freckle that's the shape of Jamaica."

"Tonisha?" asked Millicent, panicking. "Did you use Bully-Be-Gone?"

"Two days ago," said Tonisha.

"Two days ago!" Millicent almost shouted. "Has anyone else used it?"

"I don't know," said Tonisha.

"Think hard, Tonisha," said Millicent.

"I talked to Leon yesterday," said Tonisha. "But I don't know if he's used Bully-Be-Gone. He's got the flu. Bad. Stuffed-up nose and everything. He won't be back to school for a few days. Why are you interrogating me?"

"I think," said Millicent, "I think there's something wrong."

Tonisha continued as if she hadn't heard Millicent. "It's funny how a simple tune can change your outlook. A few melodious notes embroidered on a shawl of lovely lyrics and, well—I think I may be speechless. Imagine that." She stared at Millicent, but it seemed she was looking right through her. "I won't be able to do lunch today. I have plans," she added with a crazy smile, then walked toward the main building, though it seemed she could have flown she was so giddy.

Oh, this is not right, thought Millicent as she watched Tonisha disappear through the school's massive oak doorway. *Not right, not right at all.*

Nine

Students filed into the Winifred T. Langley Memorial Auditorium, huddled in groups, talking and laughing. Student assemblies generated a light mood; most kids were happy to be anyplace other than a classroom. However, Millicent trailed behind the cheery crowd, not sure if she wanted to be there or not.

She almost walked past Pollock's painting display in the foyer without noticing.

"Oh, Pollock," a deep voice said. "You're so talented. What is this one called?"

Millicent turned to see Nina Kwaikowski swooning over Pollock.

"Ming Dynasty Vase with Irises from a Sharpei's View," said Pollock, scooting away from Nina, who followed him as if she were on a leash.

Millicent ducked behind a door and watched.

"What's a sharpei?" Nina asked, inching toward Pollock.

"A wrinkled dog," Pollock said, taking a step backward.

"Pretty colors," Nina said, her nose jutting upward. "And you smell pretty, too." She circled him like a shark, her face a happy, twisted jumble of features.

Pollock caught sight of Millicent. "This is all your fault!" he shouted. He tried to bolt, but Nina grabbed his collar. "Get off me!" Pollock yelled. He wriggled free of her grasp and ran out the front door.

Nina ran after him, calling, "Pollock, Pollock!"

Oh, boy, thought Millicent. *Oh, boy, oh, boy, oh, boy.* More statement than question, she added aloud, "Am I in trouble."

Millicent waited until most of the students found seats before she entered the auditorium. She snuck into the very last row, where there were only a handful of vacant chairs. Around her, the creaking of chairs and the hum of voices gradually subsided into silence.

Huge, floor-to-ceiling windows lined the auditorium walls, and the heavy drapes that were normally drawn were tied open. Millicent looked out a window and wished she were far, far away. She saw Pollock run past with Nina at his heels. Millicent did a double take, then buried her head in her hands.

Mr. Pennystacker lumbered onto the stage, grunting as if he'd eaten a disagreeable breakfast. He adjusted his glasses and ran his fingers through the five hairs atop his otherwise bald head. Externally, his youthful angles had been rounded over time, leaving a soft, large figure. Internally, he was all sharp edges. "Welcome, students of Winifred T. Langley Middle School and good morning," he boomed.

"Good morning, Mr. Pennystacker," a few students responded.

"In celebration of a brand-new school year, I've asked some of Langely's finest students to share their talents. As you probably saw when you entered, our very own Pollock—I mean, Everett—Wong's artwork is on display. If you haven't seen it, please take the opportunity on your way out. Personally, my favorite painting is *Upside-Down Upside-Down Cake, a.k.a. Right-Side-Up Cake.*"

"Whatever," someone shouted.

"That will be enough," said Mr. Pennystacker. "Unless you'd like to meet me in my office, whoever you are." He scanned the room. Of course, the person in question didn't volunteer. "All righty, then," he stated.

"To open our festivities, Juanita Romero Alonso will

perform a selection from *Love for Three Oranges* . . . by whom, Juanita?"

"Prokofiev," said Juanita from the wings.

"Like I said. *Love for Three Oranges*," Mr. Pennystacker said. "Please welcome Juanita Romero Alonso." He gestured for Juanita to enter.

Someone sitting not far from Millicent gave an exceptionally loud cheer, but she couldn't see who it was.

Juanita strode onstage wearing a flouncy yellow dress, which garnered a few snickers from the audience. "Yellow marshmallow," someone yelled. Juanita ignored the remark and tucked her violin under her chin. She raised her bow, then started to play. Immediately, the most gorgeous sounds exploded from her violin, sending most of the kids into a quiet reverence.

A few rows from Millicent, some kids sat talking among themselves, unimpressed by Juanita's performance. Suddenly, one of the talkers was pushed from his seat onto the floor.

"Shut up!" his attacker shouted. "My Juanita's playing."

Millicent stood up to see who'd done the pushing. It was a red-faced Pollywog Jones.

Pollywog leaped over the kid who'd been pushed and ran up to the stage, as if he were at a rock concert and Juanita were a rock star. He propped his arms on the edge of the stage and rested his head on his arms, watching Juanita the whole time. Juanita stared at him and moved over a few feet, not missing a note. Pollywog moved, too, swaying his wide hips to the melody.

It was then that the laughter started. At first, Millicent didn't know why they were laughing. Then she saw it. Pollywog Jones had written with a big, fat, black marker on the seat of his faded jeans WONITA, WONITA, I ♥ WONITA. The laughter grew to a deafening pitch. Juanita looked puzzled at first, but kept playing while she ran from one side of the stage to the other. Pollywog shadowed her, which only made the crowd laugh louder.

Millicent slapped her hands over her mouth.

Thoroughly annoyed, Juanita threw her arms down, her violin swinging at her side like a dead chicken. She scanned the room as if she were looking for someone. She locked eyes with Millicent. Slowly, deliberately, she raised her bow and pointed it directly at her friend. Then she stormed off the stage in a froth of yellow chiffon.

Ten

Felicity stood at the entrance of Pinnimuk City Station, her hands in her coat pockets, her jaw sagging in awe. She'd never been to Pinnimuk City Station before. She never had any reason to go. Now she did.

People on the go from someplace to someplace else shouted orders. Businessmen and women talked on cell phones. Vacationers called to stray children. Couples said good-bye with lingering embraces. She was overwhelmed by the sheer beauty of Pinnimuk City Station and felt terribly out of place. It seemed to her that even the most average person there was more significant than she or better dressed than she, or both.

Felicity felt conspicuous, like a spot on a white table-cloth. She tidied herself as best she could by removing her hat and combing her dingy hair with her fingers, brushing off her dirty coat, and buttoning both her tattered cardigans.

She walked over to a kiosk that featured a map and fun facts about Pinnimuk City Station and studied it carefully.

"My word," she said.

The hexagonal station stood four stories high, a wonder made of imported green marble. Two-story, hand-carved statues of otters served as pillars at its six corners. It spanned two city blocks and provided bus, sky tram, gondola, and helicopter service to destinations within the city and outside it.

On the rooftop was the heliport. In the middle of the roof was a very pricey, revolving glass-domed restaurant. The fourth floor housed a So Much Stuff, So Little Time department store. Skyway Central, on the third floor, was skewered by glass tunnels. Like spokes of a wheel, they fanned out to key points in the city. Through the tunnels ran the quietest electric trams you'd ever not heard.

Felicity had seen the trams darting above her throughout the city. She'd thought that riding them would be similar to being shot from a cannon. She scratched her head. She couldn't find the bus terminals on the map.

A man stepped up to the kiosk.

"Pardon me, sir," she said to him. "Can you tell me

where the bus terminal is? I'm going south to Masonville."

The man covered his nose. "Past the river," he said, his voice muffled by his hand, and pointed to Pinnimuk River before scurrying off.

Pinnimuk River flowed through the first floor, dividing the station in half with a swath of chocolate-colored water. Gondolas bobbed on its surface and took tourists, who favored leisurely, touristy transportation, to a number of docks in the city.

Felicity looked back at the map and found Pinnimuk River. Two spectacular green glass bridges connected the north and south bus terminals. Fishing, according to the regulations posted on the map, wasn't permitted from the bridges. This didn't stop occasional sightings of mischievous kids sitting on the railings with fishing lines tied to their big toes.

A porter in a red suit and white gloves approached Felicity. Huge gold epauletts perched on his shoulders like affectionate parakeets with braided tail feathers, and he had a heavy gold whistle hanging from a cord around his neck. He seemed to be of medium age; old enough to be a father, perhaps, but not as old as she. He looked regal and well-informed.

"Sir?" she asked politely yet loudly enough to be heard over the din.

"Ma'am," he replied coldly.

"I must get to Masonville," said Felicity. "Can you tell me exactly how to accomplish that?"

The porter's eyes scanned Felicity from her splitting shoes to the tattered knit cap in her hand. She stuffed the ratty thing in her coat pocket.

"Ma'am," he said, "I'm afraid you won't be able to board the bus in that condition. Regulations, ma'am."

"Regulations?" asked Felicity in a sad and panicked tone. "But I must get home. I've got the fare." She presented her crumpled five dollar bill, ironing it flat with her palm so he could see it clearly. Money, she knew, was a language spoken by most people. She assumed her five dollar bill spoke the correct dialect.

"I'm sorry, ma'am," he said. "You'll have to move along now."

She frowned and bit her lip. She heard "move along" nearly every day—move along from the park, move along from sidewalk coffee shops, move along from the shopping mall. She was tired of it.

"I must board a bus to Masonville, young man," she said loudly.

"Please, ma'am," he said, pursing his lips. "Try not to make a scene."

He was so condescending! She stomped her foot. Rather than making the commanding thud she'd hoped for, it slapped helplessly on the marble floor as if it were a trout that had leaped from the Pinnimuk River into the station.

He grabbed her by the elbow, tugging gently.

"Where are you taking me?" she wailed. "I've a bus to

catch! I came from the sky and I've been twenty years forgetful. Just yesterday I remembered my address."

Felicity worried she sounded loony, but she was beyond upset. She had not gone through all she'd been through—forgetting her identity, surviving on the impossible streets for decades, then remembering who she was—only to be kept from finally returning home. This was not how her story was supposed to end!

The porter pulled her through the bus terminal, past gawking folks without the sense to mind their own business. They came to the large, glass front doors.

"I'm sorry, ma'am," said the porter with no trace of sincerity as he opened the door and pushed her outside.

Felicity began crying. The porter was the approximate age her child would have been, had she had one, but she'd never have raised an innocent child to be so dour an adult.

"You know," she said, wiping her nose on her sleeve, "when you were just a boy, I was famous; a human cannonball. Children for miles around came to see me soar across the circus tent's red-and-yellow-striped sky, to applaud me, to ask for my autograph. How is it that lovely children can become such ugly grown-ups?" She raised her hands to her face and sobbed into them.

The porter's eyes widened.

"You were a human cannonball?" he asked.

"Yes, son." She sniffled.

"With the circus?" he asked.

"Yes," she said, adding, "only institution I know of that has 'em."

"The Sprightly Sisters All-Woman Circus?" he asked.

Felicity looked up. "Why, yes," she answered, drying her eyes.

"You're the Fabulous Flying Felicity!" he nearly shouted.

"Yes, yes!"

"Come back inside," he said quietly.

He ushered her past onlookers toward a side room in the terminal. Once there, he unlocked the heavy wooden door and heaved it open.

Eleven

Second period class was a distraction for Millicent. Typically, history was one of her better subjects, and Mrs. Alpha was one of her favorite teachers so far this year.

But Millicent was fidgety. Bully-Be-Gone was causing major problems that she couldn't fix from her desk.

It had taken Mrs. Alpha some time to quiet her class after the assembly. After a few attempts she'd gotten everyone to stop laughing about Pollywog and Juanita.

She stood at the head of her class of sixth graders, teaching history as she often did—someone tossed out a year at random and Mrs. Alpha told the class everything that happened that year with encyclopedic accuracy. Someone always tried to trip up Mrs. Alpha by shouting out an obscure year. Today, it was 1521 and Mrs. Alpha was going on and on about Portuguese explorer Ferdinand Magellan and how he'd been murdered in the Philippines.

Millicent squirmed in her seat, her desk creaking like an old boat. She was so preoccupied, she hadn't even thought to ask Roderick, who sat in front of her, if he'd used Bully-Be-Gone. Roderick huffed at the sound of each creak of her desk. Finally, he turned around.

"Millicent," he said, "would you please stop that racket?"

His ears were fuchsia, a shade darker than his pink face.

"Huh?" she asked.

"That racket," said Roderick. "I'm trying to get an education here."

"Oh," she said.

She hadn't heard a word he'd uttered. She started tapping on her desk with a pencil, thinking of a solution, and rocking back and forth.

Roderick turned around again and gripped the back of his chair.

"Millicent," he said, "am I going to have to raise my hand, get Mrs. Alpha's attention, and ultimately get you suspended for obstruction of my educational rights?"

"Right," said Millicent blankly. She ripped a piece of paper from her binder and scribbled a possible antidote for

Bully-Be-Gone. *No, that wouldn't work.* She crumpled the paper. She ripped another piece of paper from her binder, scribbled again, wadded that one up.

"Darn it, Millicent," Roderick said, taking a deep breath. "Would you please—"

"Yes?"

"Would you please—" he said. "Would you please . . ."

Millicent finally looked at Roderick. He had a funny look on his face. His nose was wiggling and his lips were pulled across his round face in a pair of fine lines. His eyes were blissfully rolled up under his eyelids, his tiny pink fingers perched atop his chair like a row of shrimp.

Millicent thought he looked more appalling than usual.

"Pepperoni and pistachios," he said dreamily.

"What?" asked Millicent, though she had a distressing notion exactly what was going on.

"What was I saying?" he asked.

"You said, 'Would you please—'" she replied cautiously. "That was it."

"Would you please—" he repeated. He seemed confused, as if he were being forced to say something against his will. "Go out with me for pizza and ice cream after school?" he blurted.

Millicent jumped out of her seat.

"I have to go to the bathroom!" she screamed.

The whole class gasped.

"Rather badly, I assume," said Mrs. Alpha, motioning toward the door, forgoing the required hall pass.

The class burst into laughter as Millicent gathered up her things and rushed out of the classroom.

Millicent scanned the girls' room to be certain she was alone. She checked for feet under the stall doors. Empty. She did some of her best brainstorming in rooms that echoed, and it was absolutely necessary she be alone now because she'd be talking to herself.

"Okay," she said aloud. "It's okay, everything's okay." The room twanged in response.

She didn't believe herself. Everything was not okay. To begin with, Fletch Farnsworth had a crush on Tonisha Fontaine. By itself, it was news enough to make Millicent's braids stand at attention. Worse, Tonisha seemed to like him back. Even worse: the student assembly fiasco with Nina chasing Pollock and Pollywog's now famous ode-to-Juanita butt.

Worse still—if that were possible—Roderick Biggleton had made mushy faces at Millicent herself and asked her out for pizza and ice cream. The thought of it tied her stomach into uneasy knots. She could barely be in the same room with Roderick, much less consume food in his presence. Worst of all, it seemed as if Bully-Be-Gone wasn't washing off. Tonisha applied it two days ago. This meant it had survived at least two showers.

The bell rang and the hall filled with the sounds of footsteps and chatter. Millicent ducked into a toilet stall, locked the door, and sat. A couple of girls entered the bathroom.

Millicent recognized their voices immediately.

"I'm never speaking to her again," Juanita cried. "That was the height of embarrassment."

"Is this lipstick too flashy?" Tonisha asked. "I don't want to scare him off."

"What are you talking about? Scare who off?"

"I wish I had longer eyelashes."

"What?"

"Winking is better with long eyelashes. Do you have any mascara?"

"No. Masonville to Tonisha. Hello?"

"My eyebrows are good, though."

"Tonisha, what is wrong with you?"

The bell rang again, signifying the start of third period.

"I'm going to be late to orchestra practice."

"I have to wait two more classes to see him."

They shuffled out of the girls' room.

"Him who?" Juanita asked as the door closed.

Third period was under way. Millicent left the stall, went to a sink, and stared at her reflection. "You have a problem of staggering proportions on your hands . . . on . . . your . . . hands." She had put Bully-Be-Gone on her hands! She jumped toward the sink and turned on the faucet, pumped soap onto her palms from the dispenser on the wall, and started scrubbing furiously. She scrubbed her neck until there was a beard of foam dripping onto her sweater. "But it doesn't wash off," she argued with herself. The thought of creeps with crushes on her made her scour her face even harder. "Got to try . . . got to get it . . . from my head to my . . . ankles. My ankles!" She'd put Bully-Be-Gone on her ankles. "Dang it!" She kicked off her shoes, yanked off her socks, hiked up her skirt, and stuck her right foot into the sink and lathered it while hopping on her left foot. *Too awkward*, she thought. So she gripped both faucets and hoisted herself off the floor until her left foot was in the sink too, her tush hanging over the edge. Now, it was plain to see she couldn't scrub herself because she needed to hold onto the faucets to keep from falling out; so she turned, ever so slowly, so that she could rest her fanny against the wall which freed her hands to wash her ankles.

Anyone entering the girls' room at that moment might have considered normally sensible Millicent in the sink a laughable sight, but she didn't think her predicament was humorous at all. She was rubbing her skin raw, the redness beneath the mounds of bubbles looked like cuts of beef. Soap drizzled from her face as if she'd strolled through a car wash.

Suddenly Millicent's feet squirted out of the basin. She landed on her bottom in the sink with a painful smack, her legs sticking out like antennae, her bottom plugging up the basin. Water filled the sink to overflowing, spilling over the rim and flowing toward and under the door.

She was in such a state that she didn't hear the footsteps coming down the hall.

An urgent pounding at the door echoed in the girls' room. "What is going on in there?" a voice boomed. The voice belonged to Mr. Pennystacker.

"Nothing, Mr. Pennystacker," Millicent said as innocently as she could.

"The hallway is flooding," the voice said. "I'm coming in."

The door swung open.

"Miss Millicent Madding," Mr. Pennystacker exclaimed. He wedged his hands between his belly and hips and strode up to the sink. "Miss Millicent Madding," he said again. "In the sink."

"Uh-huh," said Millicent.

"May I see your hall pass, Miss Madding?" asked Mr. Pennystacker, extending his hand.

"It seems I don't have one," said Millicent, feeling rather stupid.

"Not in class, in the sink—without a hall pass. Two infractions." He positioned himself before Millicent and squatted so the two of them were at eye level, so close that Millicent could smell the greasy hair product holding his comb-over in place. "Tell me," he continued, "do you not have a shower at home?"

"Um, no, sir. I mean, yes. I mean, no," Millicent replied. "It's so difficult to answer a question worded in the negative, sir." She thought about it for a second, then said, "We do. We do have a shower."

"Then what, pray tell, is the reason for this preposterous hygienic display?" Mr. Pennystacker stared at Millicent as though through the lens of a microscope.

Millicent folded her hands in her lap, the water from the faucets running down her back, soaking into her sweater, spreading dark blobs to the front of it.

"Well, it's a mildly funny story, really," she said. "And a long one. I'd rather not bore you."

"I've got time," said Mr. Pennystacker, restoring himself to his full height. "And I love a snoozer of a tale—hear 'em all the time. Meet me in my office, pronto." He turned and walked out of the girls' room with the swagger of a Thanksgiving Day parade balloon.

In short order, Millicent was sloshing down the hall, leaving a trail of water behind her. It had taken her five minutes to get out of the sink, as she was slippery with soap. Whenever she passed a classroom, she hunched over so no one would see her through the small window at the top of each door.

A dozen questions bombarded her brain. Was she in serious trouble? What was the penalty for bathing in the girls' room sink? How quickly would her clothes dry? Had she been able to wash away the Bully-Be-Gone she'd so generously doused herself with? What was she going to tell Mr. Pennystacker?

Lists gave her a sense of control she otherwise lacked under stressful conditions, so she stopped, fumbled around in her backpack, and found a notepad and pen. A puddle of water formed beneath her. She walked a few steps, then stopped again.

"Okay," she said aloud, "who used Bully-Be-Gone?"

She scribbled: *me, Tonisha, Pollock, Juanita. Who else?* She'd handed out samples to all the Wunderkinder. That meant Leon had possibly used it. Fortunately, he was home sick. If luck were with her, Leon would return to school after the Bully-Be-Gone had worn off.

The very thought of another Wunderkinder being hounded by a bug-eyed hoodlum was enough to make her sweat, which added to her dampness. Another puddle formed beneath her, so she moved on.

Mr. Pennystacker's office was at the end of a narrow hall; his was the only door for several feet. Outside it were two long benches that normally played host to kids responsible for any assortment of disobediences and disruptions. Fortunately, there was no one sitting on them today. Millicent turned the doorknob and entered.

Behind the admittance counter, she saw an enormous light-blue wig bobbing along.

"Hello?" she asked.

The blue wig shot up from behind the counter. A couple of paper clips fell out of it. The wig belonged to Miss Bucket, Mr. Pennystacker's assistant.

"What a fright," Miss Bucket exclaimed, adjusting her wig and her glasses that had both gone askew.

"Sorry," said Millicent.

"Why, Miss Millicent Madding," said Miss Bucket, her eyebrows arched above the rims of her glasses like two alarmed cats. "You're a stranger to these parts. What brings you here?"

"Mr. Pennystacker told me to come."

"Curious. Well, sign in please," said Miss Bucket, handing Millicent a clipboard. "Now, where did I put my pen?" Miss Bucket kept a number of pens in her wig. Millicent pointed to Miss Bucket's head where she could see a ballpoint pen dangling. "Thank you, dear," said Miss Bucket. "Let's see now, red?" Millicent waited patiently while Miss Bucket dug around for the appropriately colored pen. "No, you look like a purple kind of gal," Miss Bucket said, passing Millicent a grape-scented felt-tip pen.

"Thank you," said Millicent, dripping water onto the clipboard.

"You're as wet as a slobbering hyena," said Miss Bucket. "However did that happen?"

"I was in the girls' room sink," Millicent replied sheepishly.

"Sponge bath, eh?" asked Miss Bucket with a wink. "I've tried rinsing down in the faculty ladies' room sink. It gets you nothing but odd looks." She rummaged around in her desk and produced a packet of moist towelettes. "My advice? Try these wipes. They're so—"

"Miss Bucket!" a voice blasted.

Miss Bucket screamed and jumped back. Several pencils and pens fell out of her wig and onto the floor.

Mr. Pennystacker stood in the doorway of his office, his arms folded hard and shut as tight as a bear trap. "I'd appreciate it if you'd leave me to my official advisory capacity," he growled.

"Yes, sir," said Miss Bucket breathlessly.

"And you, Miss Millicent Madding," said Mr. Pennystacker. "Follow me." He waddled into his office, hooking a beckoning finger behind him.

Millicent followed him.

"Shut the door, please," said Mr. Pennystacker, easing himself into his chair with a grunt. "And have a seat."

Millicent shut the door and plopped herself into a hard metal chair. It felt icy against her wet rear. She wanted to yelp, but didn't.

"You may begin by explaining how it is you came to be bathing in the sink," Mr. Pennystacker said gruffly, gripping his chin with his chubby hand.

"I was in the sink—"

"That's been established," said Mr. Pennystacker. His pupils became dark, small, reflective beads, like two beetles crawling around on the whites of his eyes.

"Well—" said Millicent. This wasn't going so well.

Mr. Pennystacker's face suddenly went soft, the pinch in his expression easing into a mushy grin. "Say, do you smell that?" he asked.

"Smell what?"

"That," Mr. Pennystacker said dreamily, pointing to the air around him as if he were trying to get a bird to land on his finger. "That lovely, lovely smell."

"No," replied Millicent. She'd never seen Mr. Pennystacker with such a spectacularly goofy look on his face.

"It smells like—like cinnamon buns," said Mr. Pennystacker, "and a Saint Bernard I had as a child. Her name was Magda."

"Magda?" asked Millicent. She was getting uncomfortable, less because of her wet clothing than because of Mr. Pennystacker's growing strangeness.

Mr. Pennystacker leaned back in his chair and continued as though he were alone in his office, talking to himself. "Magda," he said, staring at the ceiling. "I called her Mad Dog, though. Her favorite game was cinnamon bun diving. We had an Olympic-sized swimming pool with a diving board at my childhood home. I'd climb onto the diving board, Mad Dog behind me, sniffing at a cinnamon bun I had in my hand. I'd throw the bun as far as I could into the pool and Mad Dog would leap off the diving board and paddle her heart out to get to that bun. We'd go like this for hours. Up and down the diving board we went, in and out of the water went Mad Dog until she was utterly exhausted. My, my. What fun. What a happy memory."

Mr. Pennystacker sat for what seemed like minutes, beaming.

No wonder Mr. Pennystacker is so scary, Millicent thought. His happiest memory involved torturing a dog with a pool and breakfast pastry.

Millicent cleared her throat.

"Oh," said Mr. Pennystacker. "What are you doing here, Mad Dog—I mean, Millicent?"

"I'm, uh, I'm wet," answered Millicent. She was tempted

to remind Mr. Pennystacker why she'd been called into his office in the first place, but she thought better of it. Bully-Be-Gone seemed to be working like it was supposed to for once.

"Silly girl," Mr. Pennystacker said. "You mustn't wander about drenched. You might catch cold." He stood up, walked around to Millicent, and tenderly placed a hand on her head and patted it. "I want you to go home," he continued, escorting Millicent to the door. "Get out of those clothes, take a hot bath, and spend the day in bed, cuddled up with a warm blanket and warmer milk."

Millicent crept out of Mr. Pennystacker's office, her evaporating footprints the only evidence she'd been there.

Twelve

Felicity peeked into the room while the gilded porter held the door. Inside, metal shelves stood from floor to ceiling, each weighted with stacks of luggage. Outside, Pinnimuk City Station bustled with activity.

"Please," the porter said, gesturing for her to enter. She did and he shut the door.

"Are you going to lock me in here?" asked Felicity, feeling a little more than claustrophobic.

"No, no," he replied.

"Are you going to stow me away in a steamer trunk?"

"No, no," he said again. He pulled out a couple of suitcases from a bottom shelf. He sat on one and offered the other to Felicity. She sat without a word. "The Fabulous Flying Felicity. My, my." He took off his cap and scratched his head. "You were my very favorite performer."

"Was I?" Felicity clasped her hands together on her lap. He was a fan. She wanted to hear more about how much he'd liked her act.

"Oh, yes," he said.

"Do tell," she said. "What was it about me you admired so?"

"Your bravery," he said, "the way you made it look so effortless."

"I was pretty good, wasn't I?" asked Felicity.

"Goodness, yes. Mother and Father took me to see you every visit the circus made to town. I loved acts of extreme daring. But my personality is of the type better equipped to watch such exhibitions of courage." He paused for a moment, looking as though he were making a wish. "I collected your autographs, though," he continued. "To this day, I have them arranged in a scrapbook in order by date. In fact, I got your signature scant minutes before you went through the tent roof—my last entry under your name."

"Ah," she sighed.

"Saddest day of my life," he said.

"Mine too," she said.

She wished she could tell him she remembered him. There were so many children, though. Too many to identify their adult faces years later. Did that matter? What mattered was right now. Now, he was a grown-up child with a face full of wonder. In him, she saw the face of every child who'd ever loved her.

"Say," he said, pulling a piece of paper and pen from his chest pocket, "can I have another autograph?"

"Gladly," said Felicity, taking the paper and pen. She was almost brought to tears again, happy to have a name to sign and a fan for whom to sign it.

She signed the piece of paper and handed it to him.

He folded it carefully in two and put it in his wallet. "So, what happened to you? How can you be alive? The fall alone would've killed anyone."

Felicity told him of the events following her supposed demise.

After ripping through the circus tent, she'd hurtled through the sky for a number of minutes, Pinnimuk City stretching below her like a relief map. She truly thought all was lost. Fortunately, Pinnimuk City's annual Hot Air Balloon Festival had been taking place the same day. The sky bulged with hundreds of hot air balloons in every size and color, like a huge kaleidoscopic mattress, to break her fall. She saw one balloon in particular growing larger and larger with each fraction of a second. She didn't remember the impact, but the balloon pilot, a kindly man who went only by Ed, later told her that she'd appeared out of nowhere and came crashing into his carriage, hitting her head in the process. She'd gotten amnesia from the collision and lain unconscious for nearly an hour.

Upon awakening, she remembered nothing of her human cannonball career, of her inventor husband. Her helmet had come off when she'd torn through the tent and the polka-dotted leotard she once adored now embarrassed her.

Ed invited her to stay at his place, in a gardener's cottage on his property. In exchange for free room and board, he asked that she care for his small agricultural plot while he conducted balloon rides and trainings. She agreed since her schedule was wide open for the foreseeable future.

She lived there, on Ed's Balloonist Dude Ranch, for a year, tending his gardens and eating fresh vegetables. Over time, though, she became restless. One spring day, the weather full of promise and the vegetable seeds tucked into their soil beds, she told Ed the time had come for them to part. Ed gave her a seldom-used brown tweed suit of his and a jar of pickled beets. He bid her a teary farewell and a smiling good luck.

She wandered for the next twenty or so years, up and down the complex street system of Pinnimuk City, searching for that special house that would jog her memory. She didn't find it. Gradually, she came to accept the streets as her future and discarded her dreams of a warm fire, a place to belong, and love. Home, she came to believe, was a cardboard box, a burrow under a bridge, or a space between trash cans in an alley.

She managed to maintain her health and enjoy hot meals through the generosity of the Sisters of Routine

Kindnesses and Involuntary Thoughtfulnesses, an order of nuns who wore wool habits as soft to the touch as asphalt, and who gave the downtrodden free medical and dental exams and baked lasagna.

This was her life thus far: a series of unsavory places to rest her head, of dental torture, of free Italian food. And it would have proceeded so if it were not for the recent smells in the park. She told him that she'd been asleep on a grassy knoll, that she'd been awakened by the most marvelous smells descending from the sky. They were circus smells, love smells, smells of her past. And she inhaled them like fresh air. What was wrong had been righted simply by breathing. Her memory had returned.

"And that," she said, "is what happened."

"Remarkable," the porter said. "Astounding."

"And that," she said, "is why I must get home to my inventor. I've been gone for so long."

"We will get you there," the porter said. "Name's Garner, by the way. Garner Netterby." He reached out his hand. She took it heartily and shook it, nearly seesawing his arm off. "First, we need to get you some presentable clothing, or you won't be allowed on the bus," he said, standing.

"I've got five measly dollars," Felicity said. "I don't think I can afford an outfit." Her heart dropped. She was on the verge of crying yet again, unable to handle another obstacle.

"My dear." Garner laughed. "You are sitting in the unclaimed baggage storage room—the final resting place of all abandoned, unwanted travel accessories. Amazing what people leave behind: dresses, shoes, socks, makeup. Where the people go, why they desert their belongings is a mystery. Anyway, whatever you can find in this monstrous pile of luggage that fits you and is to your liking, you can have."

"Oh," whispered Felicity, surveying the room, awestruck, her eyes welling with tears. "How can I thank you?"

"By washing and dressing quickly," he replied. "I could get into trouble for this. Regulations state that only employees are granted access to this room. There's a shower through there." He indicated a door on the rear wall. "Now, hurry. I'll be outside guarding the entrance. Knock when you're ready."

Twenty minutes later, a rap at the door rang out. Garner, who stood at attention, leaned toward it secretively. "You done?" he asked.

"Yes," Felicity answered.

Garner opened the door. He did a double take.

"Interesting choice," he said.

"You like?" Felicity asked, doing a fashion model turn.

"Well," said Garner, thinking briefly. "Yes. Yes, I do." He laughed. "I do. Get it? I do?" he asked.

Of the garments available to her, in those mounds and mounds of totes and duffels and suitcases, Felicity had chosen a wedding dress. It was the color of a parchment scroll or breakfast tea with milk—beige, with tiny pearls cascading from the neckline down to the waist. The narrow sleeves ended in points at the wrist and the skirt was a hill of satin. She'd swept her silvery hair into a bun. Yards of matching gossamer tulle formed the veil, sprouting from a ring of silk flowers resting solidly on her head.

Layered over the wedding dress was an orange parka with a fur-trimmed hood and so many pockets it looked like an overgrown fishing vest.

"I love this dress," Felicity cooed from beneath the veil, swishing her skirt around, "and the jacket is divine. Lots of storage space."

"You gonna wear the—" Garner started to ask, pointing to the veil. "Never mind. You look stunning."

She pulled the veil back to reveal that she had done her makeup: purple eyeshadow, peach lipstick, and round pools of berry-colored blush on her cheeks.

"I picked out shoes, too," she said, lifting her skirt to show him her selection. "They kind of match my eyelids. Hope I didn't go overboard."

His eyebrows jumped at the sight of the lilac hiking boots she had on. "Not in the least."

"It's been so long since I've felt pretty," she said. "I feel magical. Absolutely magical."

"Good," said Garner, "because we're going to need a dose of magic to get you on the last bus to Masonville. C'mon."

He grabbed her by the arm and they ran together, weaving through the throngs of people, to the south ticket counter. Garner sounded his gold whistle to clear a path. People applauded as they swept past, cheering what they thought was a bride. They clattered over one of the glass bridges where Felicity stopped to wave at a gondolier. Garner urged her forward.

Soon, they stood breathless at the ticket counter.

"Nick," said Garner to the ticket agent, who was preparing to shut his gated window, "we need to get this beautiful lady a ticket to Masonville."

"But it's leaving in—" complained Nick, checking his watch, "one minute. Regulations say we can't sell tickets within five minutes of departure."

"Nick, my friend," said Garner, leaning so that his nose touched the glass window. "Regulations, schmegulations. This is urgent." Nick stared at him blankly. "It's her wedding day," he lied.

"Okay, okay," said Nick. "Don't tell anyone I did this." His fingers flew across the buttons of his ticket machine and a strip of hard paper shot out. He slid it under the glass partition. "No need to pay. It's on the house," he said to Felicity. "Have a wonderful wedding."

Garner and Felicity ran to the platform. The Masonville bus was pulling away from the boarding zone. He blew hard on his whistle and the bus screeched to a stop, then gasped. The double doors hissed open.

"Madame," he said, "your coach awaits."

She put her palm to his cheek. "I can't thank you enough," she whispered in his ear as she hugged him tightly.

"Nonsense," he said, his forehead going red. "On board you go."

Felicity hiked up her skirt, easing into the bus as though she'd worn a wedding dress every day of her life. She found a seat near a window. The bus groaned into action.

Garner stood, waving with his right hand. His chest puffed. He was proud to have played a small part in sending his boyhood heroine on the most important trip of her life. He stuck his left hand in his jacket pocket, feeling for a hanky to dab a tear from his cheek. He felt a crumpled piece of paper and he removed it. It was a five dollar bill.

From her seat on the bus, her hand pressed against the window, Felicity watched Garner get smaller and smaller as the bus backed out of the station, until he was the size of a child—a child who would grow into an exceptional young man.

Thirteen

When Millicent got home from school, she saw flashes of light coming from the basement windows and heard pops and bangs. Uncle Phineas was working. Curious about what he was doing, she snuck over to a window and peeked in. Her uncle was surrounded by rolls of tape, his head in the sink under a stream of water. She'd seen enough sinks for the day. She tiptoed across the porch, shivering in her drenched, icy-cold clothing, and turned her key as quietly as she could. She crept upstairs, showered, dressed in her fuzzy bathrobe, wrapped a towel around her head, and crawled into bed. She felt like such a failure.

A knock rattled the door.

"Millicent, is that you? Are you home?" asked Uncle Phineas. "I felt the water pressure drop. Were you showering?"

She didn't want to answer.

"Millicent?" he called again.

"Yes, Uncle Phineas," she said softly. "I'm home."

"May I enter?" he asked.

"Okay."

The door opened and in walked Uncle Phineas, daylight from the window glinting off his bald head. He'd shaved it while Millicent was in school. A strip of tape ran across the center of his head from where his hairline would be to the base of his skull.

"What's that?" she asked, pointing at his scalp.

"An experiment," said Uncle Phineas, sidling up to her bedside. He sat and continued. "A new product, Diffollicle Mohawk Tape. Orange. Think of the possibilities: stripes, geometrics, bull's-eyes, labyrinths. Why, an industrious person with a working knowledge of textiles could even do a plaid, yes?"

"That's nice, Uncle Phineas," she said glumly.

"Some reaction to a product bound to shake up the cosmetological universe," he said.

"Yeah," she said, her expression vacant.

"Will I have to tickle the source of your depression out of you?" he asked, his fingers poised, "or will you offer it freely?" She didn't reply, so he scooted her over and lay down next to her. "It must be pretty bad, yes? You're home early and you appear healthy." He knew her so well.

She didn't respond.

"Well, seeing that I'm conversing solo, I'll tell you a story which may be of assistance in what I assume is your hour of need." He gave her a sidelong glance. She smiled limply. He was silent for a moment. "Where was I?" he asked.

"You were going to tell me a story," she said. "You hadn't begun yet."

He grinned broadly. "So, you were listening," he said.

She nudged him with her elbow.

"The year was 1989," he began, propping his arms behind his head, "or was it 1984? Maybe it wasn't the eighties at all. Anyway, your mother was freshly graduated from college. Oh. It had to be the eighties. That's when she graduated, yes. I'd graduated ten years before and had started my own company, Vaccu-Matic Carpets Limited."

Millicent sat up. She'd never heard the Vaccu-Matic Carpet story before.

"I thought, and rightly so," he continued, "that vacuum cleaners were archaic mechanisms, doomed to go wherever outmoded appliances go. So I invented the Vaccu-Matic Carpet with Autosuck Technology. Instead of using a vacuum cleaner to extract dirt from your carpet, with the VMC, you simply flipped a switch and the carpet retracted dirt, in a sense. Dust, soil, and other small debris were sucked through the carpet and into a plastic bag."

"Neat idea," Millicent said.

"It did moderately well. But then your mother joined the company and added her own touch. She invented a cache system that disposed of the debris by means of a hose running directly into your trash can. Inspired by your mother's enhancement, we expected a big sales increase."

"So what happened?"

"We had instructions for the new and improved VMC professionally printed in a brochure. They were supposed to clearly state that all humans and pets should be vacated while the VMC was in use. However, as luck, or bad luck, would have it, we made the mistake of contracting the services of Mr. Cedric Cerrif, a one-eyed typesetter and printer with half a brain. Literally. Lost his right eye and half—or most of a half—of his brain in a barroom brawl."

"Oh, no," she said.

"Oh, yes," said Uncle Phineas. "Poor fellow was prone to great bouts of confusion. He printed our instructions but accidentally replaced the part about vacating people and animals with a section on baking a soufflé from a cookbook he was typesetting. Astrid and I did not proofread before the instructions went to press."

"Goodness," she said.

"That came of it, too," he said. "But badness came prior. Our first sale was to Bitter Pill Pharmaceuticals, purveyors of less-than-tasty medicinals and tonics. You can imagine how ecstatic we were at landing such an important account. Carpeting their six-story office complex in

Pinnimuk City would put us in Prosperityville for a good while."

"I'd say so." Millicent mentally estimated the total square footage of a six-story office building and multiplied that by her best guess of the square yardage price of VMC. "That was a lot of money," she added.

"Yes," he said. "If it were not for the lawsuit that ensued. We installed the VMC, adhering to our own strict guidelines, accepted a whopping check from our client, and went back to our offices and waited for word of mouth to bring us our next account. That evening, the night-shift janitor in charge of buffing and shining the Bitter Pill offices flipped the VMC switch. He didn't bother checking to see if anyone was still working because he didn't know he was supposed to. In a matter of seconds, he heard horrible screams coming from an executive's office."

"What happened?" asked Millicent, clutching her blankets to her chin.

"Your mother met your father," said Uncle Phineas.

"Wh— huh?" she asked.

"Oh, it wasn't love at first sight," he said. "Love at first sight resides in the dominion of writers, painters, and psychics. The rest of us must learn love as one must learn to operate a table saw, carefully and under supervision."

Millicent's face puckered. "I'm lost," she said.

"Yes, sorry," he said. "The janitor called us immediately. We told him to shut off the VMC, but he already had and it was still sucking. Your mother and I rushed over to Bitter

Pill's offices. This wasn't as easy as you might assume. First, my car wouldn't start. Second, we couldn't take a cab because of the taxi driver's strike. Our sole mode of transportation was a rusty old tandem bicycle that carried us about five blocks before the wheels fell off."

"What did you do?"

"We ran the rest of the way, fueled by adrenaline and an overwhelming sense of responsibility," he said, raising an eyebrow at her.

"Oh."

"When we got there, I dismantled the VMC while your mother got as close to the office in question as she could without stepping on the carpet. Fortunately, the office had a glass wall and she could see into it quite clearly. There was a man, handsomer than plain but not especially striking, wearing a white lab coat. He was stuck to the floor, hollering at the top of his lungs."

"Dad," said Millicent wistfully.

"Doctor Adair Madding, yes," said Uncle Phineas. "Long story edited for consumption, he sued us for excessive suction—which put us out of business; Adair and Astrid dated and eventually got married. End of narrative."

Millicent found that listening to Uncle Phineas's stories was very much like water-skiing: you could be going along at a decent clip for quite some time, then abruptly wipe out.

"That's it?" she asked.

"Point A to point B, yes," he answered.

"Is there a moral to this story?" she asked.

"Hmmm," he murmured, "I did say it would be helpful, didn't I?"

"You did," she said.

"Well, if I were to derive a lesson from this tale," he said, stroking his beard, "I'd say it would be that you must do everything within your power to correct your own mistakes. Your happy ending, if you are indeed entitled to one, will come of its own accord."

"Uncle Phineas," she said quietly, "I just don't know how to fix my problems—by myself." She hoped he'd offer to help, but she knew he wouldn't. It wasn't that he didn't care or didn't love her or didn't want the best outcomes for her. He was just so staunch a believer in self-reliance that he was likely to remind her she could manage without him.

Uncle Phineas sat up and inched himself to the edge of the bed.

"You're a resourceful young lady," he said, standing. "I have faith in you, yes."

He ambled to her bedroom door and exited. She thought he was well on his way to the basement lab when he popped his head back in.

"You don't even have to have a solution straight away," he said. "But you do have to try your darndest to find one." With that, he disappeared.

Millicent thought about her parents. She imagined they were cheering her on, expressing a confidence in her she didn't yet have in herself.

Madame Curie jumped onto the bed, nestled close to Millicent's face, and licked it with her rough tongue.

"Is all this fixable, M.C.?" she asked.

The feline tilted her head as if to say, Could be, could be not.

"Juanita isn't speaking to me, Pollock is mad at me, Tonisha is a space case, and Roderick . . . never mind him. I need a friend."

The cat pressed her wet nose to Millicent's cheek.

"Yechhhh, your nose is runny. Runny nose . . . runny nose!" Millicent said. "Leon! Leon is home sick. He'll talk to me." She shot out of bed, got dressed, and made a beeline to Leon's house a block away.

Millicent pounded on Leon's front door until Mrs. Finklebaum answered.

"Millicent, come in. What can I do for you?" Mrs. Finklebaum asked.

"I have to talk to Leon," Millicent said, stepping inside.

"He's sleeping. What's new, right? He has the flu. Vicious bug going around. Aches, fever, stuffed-up nose—"

"I'm sorry to bother him," Millicent interrupted, "but this is urgent."

"Oh. I see," Mrs. Finklebaum said. "Upstairs and to the left. Knock first. Brace yourself. He's covered in mentholated rub."

Millicent charged up the stairs, leaving Mrs. Finklebaum scratching her head. Millicent rapped on

116

Leon's door so hard it hurt.

"Four seventy-five!" Leon shouted in a raspy voice.

"Leon, it's me, Millicent," she said through the door.

"Come in."

Millicent entered to see Leon in bed, surrounded by wadded tissues, as if he were resting in a cloud. The smell of mentholated rub made her eyes tear.

"Pull up a chair," he said. "What are you doing here?"

Millicent grabbed his desk chair and sat. "I need advice, or I need to talk," she said. "I don't know which." She told him about the events of that morning, starting with Juanita and Pollock in the drainage hole, occasionally fanning away the smell of mentholated rub. Leon nodded, blew his nose, coughed, nodded, blew his nose, and coughed as she told her story. He ran out of tissues and asked her to get him another box from his desk, which she did. She finished by saying, "I admit it, Leon, I'm responsible for another failed invention. Bully-Be-Gone is a disaster." On the verge of tears, she took a tissue for herself in case she started crying.

"Gee, I wish I could help you, but, as you can see, I'm sick."

Millicent fanned her face. "Don't you at least have any advice for me?"

Leon propped himself up on one elbow. "I always find that when I'm in trouble, telling the truth helps a lot."

"The truth is scary," Millicent said. "Maybe I can find a way around it." She fanned her face again.

"Why do you keep doing that?" Leon asked. "Do I stink?"

"Uh, yes," Millicent said. "Of mentholated rub."

"My mom must have put some on me while I was sleeping."

"You can't smell it?"

"No. My nose is plugged."

"I'm sorry, Leon." She handed him another tissue, which he brought to his bright red snout. Millicent yelped. "That's it! Your nose. That's it!" She sprung from the chair.

"My nose is it?" Leon asked.

"Yes!" Millicent nearly hollered. "Your nose is going to get me out of this mess. Thank you, Leon. Thank you, thank you, thank you." She moved forward to his bedroom door. "Thank you for your nose! Feel better!" she called out as she ran down the stairs.

Fourteen

Millicent ran home from Leon's house, inspired by his clogged sinuses. She stopped before the basement lab door to catch her breath. She knew what had to be done. She had to find a way to keep Nina, Pollywog, Fletch, and Roderick from smelling Bully-Be-Gone.

"All I have to do is find a way to plug their noses. I could put foam earplugs in their nostrils. No, too gross. I couldn't even get close enough to them to—never mind. Unless I made a pair of extending tongs that . . . no." She tapped her lips with her forefinger, concentrating. "Wait a second . . ." She thought once more about Leon, lying in bed, unable to smell the mentholated rub his mother had put on him, his sinuses clogged. "Yes! That's it!" As she unlocked the lab door, Madame Curie appeared from a flower bed and followed Millicent into the lab.

Millicent found a handwritten note on a lab table. Uncle Phineas had left it there. It said he would be at an inventor's meeting until well after dinner. Millicent set it aside, somewhat relieved he wouldn't be home for a while. She knew he'd disapprove of an invention that plugged noses. Inventors were supposed to improve people's lives. But wouldn't she make her friends' lives better if she could get the bullies to leave them alone? *Yes*, she reasoned. She had work to do. She snapped on a pair of rubber gloves.

She labored late into the night, measuring fluids, sifting powders, and mixing them together. She added them to a green bottle and shook it hard. The contents bubbled, then settled.

Then she supplemented the concoction with her secret ingredient: Tickle Tonic. To make Tickle Tonic, she'd modified the Propulsion Lotion she used in Bully-Be-Gone by blending in every allergen she could get her hands on: dust, pollen, pepper, and dander from Madame Curie. According to her theory, once molecules of Tickle Tonic were lodged in someone's nose, they would jiggle until only one response was possible.

I'll call it Hooky Spray, she thought. After all, it would be perfect for kids who want their parents to think they're sick so they can stay home from school. Not that Millicent would ever try such a thing.

She smiled at the bottle, satisfied. Hooky Spray would make its target sneeze, propelling Bully-Be-Gone out of both nostrils, then it would plug his or her nose. In effect, Hooky Spray would give the symptoms of the flu without the discomfort.

"How will I know if this is effective?" she pondered.

Madame Curie prodded Millicent's shirt with her nose as if to tell Millicent she wanted to play.

"Not now, M.C.," Millicent said as she uncapped the spray bottle.

The cat jumped at the bottle, batting it out of Millicent's hand. It fell and rolled across the lab table.

"No, M.C.!"

Madame Curie chased the bottle, swatting at it as if it were a mouse. It tumbled off the table and into a waste-paper basket, where it landed top down. Madame Curie lunged into the garbage—into a cloud of Millicent's new invention.

"Oh, no!" Millicent yelled. She reached for a filtration mask and clapped it onto her face. "M.C., are you okay?"

By then, Madame Curie had already scrambled out of the trash can, knocking it over in the process, and had wedged herself into a corner under the table.

Millicent had never tested any product on Madame Curie. Animal testing just wasn't nice. Besides, recently, on the television news program, *40 Minutes Plus Commercial Breaks*, she saw a segment about LAMA, League Against

Meanness to Animals. LAMA was an organization of activists. They went to great lengths to seek out people who wore fur coats or tested cosmetic products on animals. They did horrible things to those people. A month ago, LAMA broke into a cosmetics lab and freed all the test rabbits, but not before tying up the lab technicians and gluing cotton balls to the ends of their noses.

LAMA had spies everywhere, so Millicent peered out of the lab blinds. She saw nothing, the street outside stood dark and empty. *Good*, she thought. She didn't need a cotton ball glued to her nose.

She turned her attention back to Madame Curie. "What a stroke of luck," she said. She felt bad feeling good about the cat getting squirted, but now she didn't have to find a way to try out her invention. The cat had become her guinea pig.

She crouched under the table. "M.C., let me see you," she pleaded.

Madame Curie cowered on her haunches, a faint thread of mucus seeping from her nose. She let out three, tiny cat sneezes—*pyew, pyew, pyew*.

Millicent got an idea. The Robotic Chef had a microphone in the lab. She ordered a scoop of tuna. "Scooooop of tuuuuunaaaa," she said, enunciating as clearly as she could. Seconds later, a scoop of tuna on a saucer appeared in the chute through which meals were delivered.

"How about that?" Millicent asked no one in particular. She'd expected any food except tuna.

She placed the tuna on her desk and waited. If her potion worked, then Madame Curie wouldn't smell the tuna and would stay hidden. The cat eventually fell asleep under the table.

The next morning, Millicent showed up a few minutes early to first period with Hooky Spray in her pocket and only one plan in her head: getting within firing range of Nina, Pollywog, and Fletch. She didn't know yet how she'd pull it off.

She eased into her chair, deep in thought. Mr. Templeton, her English teacher, stopped writing on the chalkboard.

"Millicent, you're early," Mr. Templeton said, fluffing his skirt. "I can always depend on your hunger for knowledge." He gave a spin, his dress mushrooming big and black. "Guess who I am today."

"Ermengarde Rhimehoggen," Millicent said, barely looking up. "Masonville's renowned poetess—born 1879, died 1932."

"Can't pull the taffeta over your eyes," Mr. Templeton said.

It was the first Greats of Literature day of the school year, which occurred once a month and for which Mr. Templeton dressed as famous authors. Today, his outfit consisted of an expansive hat decorated with stuffed birds, much like the hats Ermengarde wore in her day, along with an authentic, puffy-sleeved, turn-of-the-century dress dotted with matching fabric rosettes. Millicent glanced at his back and saw he was too big for the costume. An eye-shaped opening where the buttons were unable to close revealed his white T-shirt. She smiled, then got back to scheming.

Tonisha's seat was in the next row to Millicent's right. Beyond that, another row over and back one seat, was Fletch Farnsworth's desk—perhaps near enough for Millicent to squirt him with Hooky Spray.

Students began to file into class. As soon as most of them caught sight of Mr. Templeton, they laughed.

Tonisha walked in and exclaimed, "Ermengarde Rhimehoggen! My favorite." She sat at her desk, clasping her hands. "Oh," she said, noticing Millicent, "I didn't see you. Today is going to be spectacular, isn't it?" Millicent looked into her eyes and saw a stranger.

Fletch walked into the classroom and howled at Mr. Templeton. Tonisha grinned as Fletch shuffled past her. He paused, took a deep breath, and blushed. "Hi, Tonisha," he said. Tonisha mumbled something back, then whispered to Millicent, "Today is going to be better than spectacular now that my Fletchie is here."

Millicent's stomach churned. She thought she might barf. *Fletchie? The same person who used to reach across the aisle and unravel your headwrap?*

"Settle down, everyone," Mr. Templeton said.

"Tonisha, I have to talk to you after class," Millicent said.

124

Tonisha waved at Fletch.

"Pssst, Tonisha," Millicent said.

Tonisha giggled at Fletch, who swooned at her, his nose poked high.

"Hey, Tonisha," Millicent said, louder.

"Order!" Mr. Templeton boomed. He stared Millicent down over the top of his glasses. "Millicent, I'm surprised at you." Millicent faced front. Mr. Templeton pursed his lips and continued. "This morning I will read Ermengarde Rhimehoggen's poignant poem 'My Heart Is a Delta and You Are a Boulder Blocking Its Left Ventricle.'" He hoisted himself onto a high stool. "Discussion to follow." He began reading in a soft, lilting voice.

Millicent had been looking forward to Mr. Templeton's impersonations. While other students laughed at him, Millicent understood he was creating an illusion—a sense of being in the presence of a literary giant. Today, she had a more important agenda. She glanced at Tonisha in time to see Fletch pass her a note. Tonisha reached back and took it. Millicent imagined it said something nauseating like "You're cute" or "I like you" or "You smell good."

Tonisha unfolded the note, read it, sighed, and fanned herself with it.

Millicent gulped. She had to put a stop to this. She reached in her pocket and pried the cap off the bottle of Hooky Spray with her thumb. How could she get near enough to Fletch to mist him? She spied the pencil sharpener mounted to the wall near his desk. Impulsively, she raised her hand. "Mr. Templeton?" she asked.

"Yes, Millicent?" Mr. Templeton replied in his Ermengarde Rhimehoggen voice.

"Um, may I sharpen my pencil?"

"Whatever for?" Mr. Templeton asked, dropping his impersonation. "I'm right in the middle of a poem."

"It's—it's so rich with meaning, I feel like—uh—like I have to take notes," Millicent lied.

"In that case, sharpen away," Mr. Templeton said, beaming.

Millicent got up and walked toward the pencil sharpener, her palms sweating. She circled around Fletch's desk. Her plan was to sharpen her pencil with one hand while aiming her Hooky Spray at Fletch with the other. She stuck her pencil in the sharpener. *Whrrrrshhh.* She extracted the green bottle from her pocket. *Whrrrrshhhh.* She pointed the bottle at Fletch. *Whrrrrshhh.* She bit her lip. *Whrrrshhh.* She squinted. *Whrrrshhh.* Her forefinger tensed. *Whrrrshhh.*

"Millicent!" Mr. Templeton boomed. "It must be a nub by now."

Millicent was so startled by Mr. Templeton, she inhaled sharply as her finger clamped down on the atomizer top, not realizing she had it facing the wrong way. A pouf of Hooky Spray assaulted her nose and open mouth. "Oh, no! Oh, no!" She gagged. She stomped in place, waving her hands in front of her face.

"It's only a pencil," Mr. Templeton said.

Millicent let out three huge sneezes. "AAAH-CHOO! AAAH-CHOO! AAAH-CHOO!" She felt her sinuses fill until she could hardly breathe. "AAAH-CHOO," she blasted again. *Oh, dear,* she thought.

"GROSS!" shrieked a girl sitting nearby.

"NASTY!" screamed another.

Millicent put her sleeve to her nose. Tonisha stared at her, aghast.

Mr. Templeton shot out of his chair. "Millicent," he said, "you are to go home immediately before you make everyone sick."

"No," Millicent said, her voice muffled by her sleeve. "I'm fine."

"Get your things and go home. Now," Mr. Templeton demanded.

Millicent returned to her desk and clumsily gathered her books, papers, and backpack, trying to keep her sleeve over her nose the whole time. "Meet me by the fountain," she managed to whisper to Tonisha before leaving English class red-faced.

Tonisha arrived at the Winifred T. Langley Memorial Fountain within fifteen minutes, brandishing a wooden hall pass.

"I had to wait until the hubbub died down before I got permission to leave," Tonisha huffed. "That was mortifying."

"Do you have a tissue?" Millicent asked.

"You almost got me in trouble," said Tonisha rolling her eyes.

"I had to talk to you," Millicent said, which was partly true.

"About?"

Millicent swallowed hard against the truth coming out. "Fletch," she blurted.

"What about Fletch?" asked Tonisha, looking concerned.

"He—it—" Millicent stuttered. She didn't know how to approach the subject. How could she tell Tonisha that Fletch's affection wasn't genuine? If she told Tonisha the truth, she ran the risk of breaking Tonisha's heart. After all, Tonisha believed Fletch liked her and, for some unknown reason, Tonisha liked him back. If Millicent didn't tell her the truth, Bully-Be-Gone would sooner or later wear off and Tonisha's heart would be broken anyway. Then there was Hooky Spray. Millicent could wait for another chance to use it on Fletch. She decided Tonisha deserved the truth. "It's not real. Fletch doesn't really—"

Just then, Fletch appeared, a hall pass in his hand.

"Hi, Tonisha," he said shyly.

Tonisha suddenly became coy, batting her eyelashes, her hands clasped behind her back. Millicent frowned. What was Tonisha trying to do? Make her ill?

"Hi, Fletch."

Fletch and Tonisha locked eyes, oblivious to Millicent's presence. A full minute went by before Fletch saw Millicent sitting there. "Oh, hi, Millicent," Fletch said.

Fletch never said hi to Millicent unless it was attached to the word "freak." She was immediately suspicious. "Hi, Fletch," Millicent said reluctantly, fondling the green bottle in her sweatshirt pocket. If she could only get him to lean closer.

Fletch smiled at Tonisha, turned toward Millicent, and said, "That was pretty funny, what you did in class."

"Humor was not my intention," mumbled Millicent, as she wiped her nose. She couldn't help but notice he was staring at her in the most peculiar fashion. He glanced at Tonisha, then her, as if he were confused.

"Did I say funny?" asked Fletch. "I think I meant to say 'cute.' You're cute when you sneeze."

Tonisha glowered.

Cute? thought Millcent. *Gross.* The last person she wanted calling her cute was Fletch Farnsworth. The truth dawned on her. He was responding to the Bully-Be-Gone on her. She eased the green bottle out of her pocket with one hand, covering it with the other. *Closer*, she thought.

He grinned at Millicent, his face inching toward hers. "Has anyone ever told you that you smell like—like freesias and warm bread?"

Millicent brought the bottle higher until it was level with her chin.

Tonisha glared hotly. "What?" she asked. She didn't wait for an answer. "What?" she shouted.

Millicent lost her nerve and stuffed the bottle back in her pocket.

Tonisha's body trembled, her headwrap jiggling like a pillar of pudding. "*I* smell like freesias and cornbread—*I* smell like freesias and cornbread." Tonisha stamped her foot.

"Warm bread," both Millicent and Fletch corrected.

"Oh, fine," growled Tonisha. "They're in cahoots."

Millicent froze. *Oh, my*, she thought. *Getting worse!*

"Is this what you wanted to talk to me about, Millicent?" asked Tonisha, her voice low and dangerous, her headwrap swaying like a cobra. "You have crossed the line—crossed the line." She drew a line on the concrete with the toe of her shoe. "Here's the line, Miss Girly Thing. And you have crossed it."

"But—but," Millicent stammered.

Tonisha spun on her heels and stormed off, talking to herself. "I want to talk to you, she says. I want to talk to you—I want to talk to you. About what? About stealing your Fletchie, that's what. Just gonna snatch your Fletchie away like that. I am *so* through with you."

Fletch looked at Tonisha, then Millicent, then back at Tonisha. Finally, as if he'd made the hardest decision in his life, he ran after Tonisha, hollering her name.

"Tonisha," Millicent whispered. "You can't leave."

Millicent sat down at the fountain's edge and heaved a sigh that seemed to start at her ankles. She reviewed the events of the past two days; bullies had crushes on her friends because of her invention, the very pink Roderick Biggleton had a crush on her, she'd been caught soaping herself in the girls' room sink, and she'd been to the principal's office. Juanita wasn't speaking to her, and, worse, now her best friend wasn't speaking to her. To top it all off, she had a solution in her pocket but couldn't get close enough to the bullies to use it.

"Could my life get any worse?" she asked herself.

She pivoted to her right and considered the bronze likeness of the Bendable Francine Tippit, a.k.a. Winifred T. Langley. She'd never noticed before, but she and Francine had so much in common. They were both brilliant yet accident prone and they were both in compromising positions.

"Could my life get any worse?" she asked again, this time directing the question to Francine.

The statue didn't answer her, of course, but if Francine were so empowered—animated by a life force or perhaps a complex system of cogs and wheels and artificial intelligence—she might have replied. Craning and creaking her metallic neck toward Millicent, she would have winked a horrible, high-pitched, metal-on-metal wink. She would have grinned a brassy grin and said in the raspy voice of a person who hadn't spoken in years, "Why, yes, Millicent dear. From where I'm sitting, I'd say your life can get significantly worse."

Fifteen

As the bus rattled along the highway, Felicity breathed two spots of fog on the window. She drew a face on each of them with her forefinger, a man's face and hers. They evaporated, leaving the countryside scenery whizzing by.

"You don't know who's touched that window before you—it could be germy," said a thin woman sitting in front of her, across the aisle. She'd been watching Felicity.

"I'm sure it's clean," Felicity said.

The woman made a tart expression, as if she'd sucked on a lemon, then buried her face in a book.

"They look clean to me," said a young voice.

"Yup, clean," said an identical voice.

Felicity turned to face twin boys who appeared to be traveling alone. They took turns drawing on their window, their fingertips leaving grimy streaks.

"What are your names?" Felicity asked.

"Clay," said one boy.

"Cleon," said the other.

"Clay and Cleon, it works better if you breathe on it first," Felicity said. "Like this." She breathed a patch of mist onto her window and drew a stick-figure dog.

"Really," said the thin woman, looking up and over her shoulder, "how unhygienic—breath *and* fingerprints."

The bus pulled into a quaint station, spitting itself to a stop. "Windy Mill Township," the bus driver called.

No one got off, but one man got on the bus. He wore a piggishly pink, ill-fitting leather suit. On his face, a plastic pig's nose attached to an elastic strap hid his real nose.

"And you are?" he asked the bus driver.

"Anne," she replied.

"I suppose I don't need to introduce myself, as you probably recognize me," he said.

Anne shook her head.

The man huffed and made his way down the aisle. With a curt nod, he acknowledged a passenger dressed as a cowboy and a serious-looking man in a suit, saying, "No autographs, please."

Felicity didn't know who he was. She craned her neck to see if there were paparazzi snapping photos at the bus station—she remembered the nuisance of the paparazzi from her human cannonball days—but it stood empty.

"Do you mind?" he asked, gesturing toward the empty spot next to her.

"Not at all," she said and patted the seat.

The bus burped into motion again.

She studied him carefully. His suit had patches sewn to it that advertised various pork products. On his sleeve alone there were three: Fatty Patty Pork Patties, Sizzle Queen Bacon, and Better-Left-Unsaid Sausage Links. He was also wearing a heavily padded shoulder harness. He grinned at Felicity, which she thought was hysterical considering his swinish nose. She didn't want to seem rude, so she stifled her laugh.

"Getting married?" the man asked.

"No, I'm not getting married," she said, covering her mouth.

"Odd get up for someone not taking vows," he said.

Odd get up? She clenched her teeth to keep from laughing.

"I take it you're not a fan of the races," he said, clearly detecting her wanting to guffaw.

"Races?"

"The Piggy five hundred," he said. "NASPIG."

"Oh?"

"I'm quite famous, actually," he said. "On the piggy-back racing circuit, that is. I'm a professional racer. My name is Boris."

"Pleased to meet you, Boris. I'm Felicity."

They shook hands, then faced forward. Felicity thought they were through talking, but her gaze kept creeping over to his patches. *Why does he have pork product labels on his clothes?* she thought.

"They're my sponsors," Boris said, as if he'd heard her unasked question.

"Sponsors?" She had no idea what sponsors were.

"Sponsors," he echoed, "are folks who pay you to display their logos on your uniform. If you're famous, as I am, they pay you lots for the privilege."

"Why?"

"Because customers will see the logos and rush out to the refrigerated aisle of their local grocery store and buy boxes and boxes of Fatty Patty Pork Patties, for example," he said.

Felicity considered how that worked. Try as she might, though, she couldn't picture being driven to buy bacon or sausage because she'd seen a patch on a celebrity's outfit. Then again, she hadn't been grocery shopping for many a year, so she reckoned it was possible there were people around who were so easily persuaded.

There were other things about Boris that didn't make sense.

"Yes," she said, after a moment, staring at his sleeve. "But if you're running around a track, how can people see these tiny patches?" She poked the Better-Left-Unsaid Sausage Links insignia on his arm. She focused on his nervous little eyes. "Besides, if they pay you so much money, why are you riding the bus?" she asked pointedly.

"Two very astute questions," he said, avoiding her stare. "To the second, I will say that I am deathly afraid of driving—speed, you know, it's a dangerous thing. To the first, I will say—umm—that—uhh—all professional piggyback racers wear patches, which show up quite nicely in publicity photographs. Yes, yes, that's right." He slapped his hands on his thighs as if he'd made up a clever answer on the spot.

Felicity frowned. "A racer afraid of speed?" she asked, cocking her head.

Boris examined his wristwatch. "Haven't we reached Masonville yet?" he asked.

"You wouldn't happen to have one of those publicity pictures on you, would you?"

"You are full of meddlesome questions," he snapped.

"A bit touchy are we?" she asked.

Boris said nothing and stared ahead. This was fine by Felicity. She was in too good a mood to converse with a grouch. She turned to watch the countryside change gradually from bright emerald farming land into foothills that pleated themselves at the base of the Curmudgeonly Mountains.

The Curmudgeonly Mountains are named for the effects their hazardous cliffs have on folks. Each peak has seven-hundred-foot-high granite walls on its western face. The cliffs wind past a valley before cascading into the sea where they form a peninsula called Cape Curmudgeon. A narrow road bends and coils along the tops of the slab walls and makes everyone who travels them edgy and cranky, common character traits of curmudgeons. When one finally makes it through Curmudgeonly Mountain Pass, seven miles from Masonville, he or she is sure to be in a rotten mood.

As the bus climbed the first of the Curmudgeonly Mountains, Felicity wondered how Boris would fare on the treacherous leg of the trip still to come, given he was already as snippy as snippy could be. His hands were pulsing tensely, leaving sweaty palm prints on his pink leather pants.

Otherwise, the journey was going well. There had not been any rain and winter was several months away, so the road was dry. An hour later, they had made it past the highest pinnacle and were on the final downward slope. Felicity strained to catch a glimpse of Masonville. She couldn't see it yet, but she was happy nevertheless. She hummed to herself. Her happily ever after was drawing near.

Then the bus driver screamed.

Sixteen

The lunch bell rang, jolting Millicent out of a daze. She shuffled out of math class to the cafeteria, alone and downtrodden. Classroom doors opened and the hallway swelled with kids, laughing and talking, going to their lockers to retrieve their lunches. Millicent watched them. They seemed like an animated collage of friendship from which she'd been cut out.

She stopped by the student bulletin board and wiped her nose on a streamer of toilet paper she'd gotten from the girls' room. A bright yellow sheet of paper grabbed her attention. It read:

138

MASONVILLE YOUTH TALENT EXTRAVAGANZA

at Lulu Davinsky's Diamond Theater,
this Friday at 3:30 P.M.
Come see your peers Juanita Romero Alonso,
Tonisha Fontaine, and ~~Everett~~ Pollock Wong compete in
their respective categories for the titles of
Masonville's most talented kids.

A girl who Millicent recognized but didn't know paused by the bulletin board. "Are you going to that?" she asked.

"I don't know if I'd be welcome," Millicent said.

"Aren't they your friends?" the girl asked.

"I'm not sure."

"Not sure? They're either your friends or they're not." The girl shrugged and bounced off.

"I'd like to go," Millicent said to herself.

She went over to her locker a few yards away and hovered there for a second, unsure what to do with herself. Tonisha's locker was three to the left. They usually met there before going to lunch together. She thought about waiting for Tonisha. "Oh, who am I kidding?" she asked. She put her books away and moved on.

Inside the cafeteria, she found a seat in the farthest corner from the entrance and sat down to unpack her lunch. She'd asked the Robotic Chef to make a bologna sandwich and it had actually made a bologna sandwich—a bologna sandwich with strawberry jelly, but a bologna sandwich nonetheless. She took a bite out of it. Her nose was still stuffed, so the sandwich tasted like paper pulp. She set it down and looked around the room.

Millicent watched Pollock and Juanita come in and look around nervously. They sat four tables away from her at the Wunderkinder's normal table. Millicent could barely hear them over the din. She cupped her ear with one hand and covered her face with the other.

What am I doing? she thought. *I should just talk to them.* Leon had told her the truth helped. Perhaps his advice was the answer after all. She got up and walked to their table. The closer she got, the clearer their voices became.

"I couldn't practice last night," Juanita complained. "Pollywog came over to my house and sang along outside my bedroom window. Off-key, no less."

Pollock got an apple out of his lunch bag. "Yeah, well, Nina called me six times last night," he said between bites. "I couldn't get any painting done."

"I'm never speaking to Millicent again," Juanita said.

"I know! I've had it with her inventions," Pollock said. "Why doesn't she take up knitting or something?"

Millicent halted. Hearing these words come from her friends' mouths made her blood run cold.

"Yeah," Juanita replied. She raised a potato chip toward her mouth, but something stopped her hand in midair. "Hey, let go!" she yelped.

Pollywog had appeared out of nowhere and had latched onto Juanita's wrist. Nina had Pollock by the arm, too. Millicent scampered back to her table and hid her face behind her hand again.

"What are you doing?" Pollock growled, struggling to free himself from Nina's big hand.

Millicent peeked between her fingers.

Both Nina and Pollywog got on their knees. Nina smacked the gum she was chewing. "Me and Pollywog are here to, uh . . ." She removed the gum from her mouth and kneaded it with her thumb and forefinger. Pollywog did the same with his. "Me and Pollywog . . ."

"It's Pollywog and I, not me and Pollywog," Pollock corrected.

"You and Pollywog what?" Juanita asked impatiently.

"We don't have real rings," Pollywog said.

"We hope these will be good enough," Nina said.

Millicent thought she might gag.

"You're gonna marry me," Nina said, wrapping her gum around Pollock's ring finger.

Pollock cringed. "Yyyyyeeeccchhhh."

"You're supposed to ask," Pollywog instructed Nina. "Like this: 'Juanita, will you marry me?'" He tugged his gum with his teeth and fingers into a strip and wound it around Juanita's finger.

Millicent clutched at her neck. She suddenly remembered the fake wedding Nina, Fletch, and Pollywog had staged on the playground a couple of years before. Nina married Pollywog and Fletch presided, having borrowed his dad's ministerial collar. Nina had brought two bags of rice, courtesy of her father, who owned the granary in the center of town. Millicent and the rest of the Wunderkinder watched from a safe distance, trying not to fall on the blacktop in fits of laughter. At the end of the ceremony, Nina heaved one of the heavy sacks of rice at Pollywog because he had said, "I do take this dork to be my wife." It knocked him off his feet. As further punishment, Nina had led him around school on a dog collar and leash for an entire week, until they finally divorced.

Juanita's face blanched as she watched Pollywog drape her finger in chewing gum. "Oh, oh, oh, oh, oh," she panted, fighting to wrest her hand from Pollywog. "EEEEEE, YUCK!" She kicked her feet and screamed like a wild creature. Breaking free, she jumped up, tore the gum off her finger, grabbed her violin, and ran screaming out of the cafeteria. Pollock bolted free, too, and flew in Juanita's wake, his portfolio banging against his leg. A few of the students who sat nearby were laughing.

"That went pretty good," Pollywog said. "Wasted my gum, though."

"You fool," Nina said. "That did not go good. It's Plan B now."

"We have a Plan B?" Pollywog asked.

"You have a Plan B?" Millicent asked so quietly only she could hear herself.

"*I* have a plan B," Nina barked at Pollywog. "*You* do what I say. Come on, let's go get Fletch. Tomorrow afternoon it all goes down. Pollock, Juanita, and Tonisha will have no choice but to marry us." She took Pollywog by the ear and dragged him from the cafeteria.

Tomorrow afternoon? Millicent's mind raced, trying to imagine what Nina had up her long, long sleeve. Obviously, the bullies couldn't really marry the Wunderkinder, but an interference of any kind could throw Pollock, Juanita, and Tonisha off for the extravaganza competition. Millicent gulped down her last bite of bologna-and-strawberry-jelly sandwich that skidded past the lump in her throat like a go-cart over a speed bump.

She had to put a stop to Nina's Plan B before it ruined her friends' most important day.

Seventeen

"**A** bear! A bear!" Anne the bus driver shrieked. She grappled with the steering wheel as she tried to keep control of the bus.

Brakes screeched, and the bus lurched as if it had tested the length of a very short leash. Then it swerved to the right in a wide, shuddering arc. *Umph, umph, umph*, the wheels went as they tried to grip the road. Boris slid on the seat, crushing Felicity. People on the other side of the bus grabbed onto the seats in front of them. Some toppled into the aisle.

Boom! The bus jolted and wheezed to a stop.

The passengers scarcely had a millisecond to regain their wits before the creaking and tilting began. It was as if the bus were a giant seesaw, whining as it tipped forward and back, tottering on the edge of the most notorious Curmudgeonly cliff: Consternation Precipice.

The name was inspired by the granite wall's anxiety-causing shape. From its base, it sloped outward and upward for five hundred feet. At the top, it jutted out, forming a twenty-foot extension. Anyone unfortunate enough to be standing—or in this case balancing—on the ridge would be mortified to find he or she could not see the bottom of the cliff.

"Everyone to the rear of the bus!" yelled the driver. People scrambled toward the last row, panting and yelping. The bus skidded a foot toward the ravine. "Slowly, slowly," she hissed. "For Pete's sake, slowly."

In her human cannonball days, Felicity had not been afraid of heights, but this was different. There was no net to catch her, no crowd applauding her now; only a whole lot of sky, the green valley hundreds of feet below, and Pinnimuk River threading its way through the valley. She thought she was going to be sick. She tried to climb over Boris who was himself struggling to get into the aisle.

"Get off me," complained Boris, swatting her away. "I have a bad back."

Felicity clambered instead over the seat behind them in a flurry of wedding dress.

As each person made it to the rear, the bus slowly

righted itself until it was tenuously level again. The seven passengers and the bus driver huddled together in a nervous mass. The cowboy twiddled his handlebar mustache. He took off his hat and wiped his brow with a red handkerchief. The thin woman patted her heart, exhaling noisily, her lips rounded into an O. The man in the suit sat in the corner, clutching his briefcase, his heels tapping a nervous rhythm. The twins sat quivering, their arms lashed around one another. Felicity squatted on the floor, glaring at Boris, and the bus driver had her head between her knees.

"Well," Felicity finally said, "that was close."

The bus driver raised her head, looked out the window, and gasped. "You spoke too soon, ma'am."

Their troubles weren't over. Outside, sniffing the tires, was the bear who'd caused the accident. It rocked to and fro, its glistening black coat catching the light and quivering in bluish waves. It sniffed its way up the side of the bus until it was standing on its haunches, then smushed its nose into the window, licking the glass. The bus driver recoiled, gagging on a suppressed scream.

"We can shoot it with our slingshots," offered the twins in unison, pulling wishbone-shaped weapons from their back pockets.

"No," Felicity whispered. "It can't see."

"How can you be sure?" asked Boris.

She pointed at the creature's smoky gray eyes. "Cataracts," she said. "Had 'em once myself. The Sisters of

Routine Kindnesses and Involuntary Thoughtfulnesses removed them—with the help of an eye doctor."

"I do believe you're correct," said the wispy woman, squinting at the bear while keeping a healthy distance from the window. "The word 'cataract' means curtain of water, which aptly describes the absorption of water on the eye's lens—a common occurrence among the elderly. This results in a clouding of the vision—"

"A blind bear?" asked the cowboy.

"It would be inaccurate to say it can't see us entirely, although it is possible the disease has advanced that far. I'd have to get a closer look—which I won't."

"What are you?" asked the man in the suit, twisting his tie. "An optometrist?"

"An eye doctor?" the wispy woman asked. "No. A modest librarian."

"I feel so much safer," Boris said.

"As to whether the bear is hungry or not," the librarian said, ignoring him, "we are nearing winter. In order to survive an extensive hibernation, it would have to consume ample amounts of food."

"In other words, an eight-person dinner," said the bus driver as she inched away from the window.

"All righty, missy," said the cowboy. "Let me recap in plainer terms: we've got an old, visually impaired bear who wants to eat us."

"Precisely," the librarian said.

"Could we be lucky enough to have a big game hunter

on this bus? A soldier? A wrestler?" asked Boris. "Nooooo. We get a librarian."

"This, coming from a man in a pink leather suit embellished with pork advertisements," said the librarian, folding her arms.

"You—" threatened Boris, wagging a finger at her. "You have 'bear appetizer' written all over your face."

"Stop it!" shouted Felicity. "We're all frightened. Frightened people say stupid things. We need to be smart."

"The bride is right," said the man in the suit. "Does anyone have a phone?"

Both the librarian and bus driver raised their hands.

"Problem solved," said the man in the suit. "We'll just call the police. Where are your phones?"

The librarian and bus driver looked at each other.

"It's in my purse," said the librarian, "which slid over there." She pointed to the front of the bus. Lying near the driver's seat was a floral-print handbag that matched her dress.

"Mine's up there, too," the bus driver said quietly.

"Oh, great," Boris grumbled.

"Then the lightest, thinnest person will fetch it," the man in the suit said, "or else we'll go crashing into the valley."

"That would mean either the librarian or one of the twins," said the cowboy, stating the obvious.

"Waaaahhh," Clay and Cleon bawled upon hearing they'd been volunteered for the dangerous mission, their faces going bright red. They pounded their fists on their thighs, stomped their feet, and started yelling over each other. "We don't want to! You can't make us! We want to go home!" Felicity tried to calm them by talking reason to them. She explained that everyone's lives depended on their courage. She told them it would be a very simple matter of crawling slowly and gently to the front of the bus, getting a phone, and coming back as slowly and gently as before. But her soothing, persuasive tone wasn't helping. They screamed louder. They screamed so loud, in fact, that the noise seemed to annoy the bear, who'd begun hitting the bus with its paws. Afraid the animal would dislodge the vehicle and send them plummeting hundreds of feet, Felicity stopped trying to persuade the small boys. They sniffled themselves quiet.

"Well," said Boris, "I guess that leaves the librarian."

Everyone turned to see her reaction.

"Oooohhh, no," she said flatly.

"Why not?" asked the man in the suit.

"I'm verminophobic."

"What-a-who-zic?" asked Boris.

"Verminophobic," she replied. "Afraid of germs. Just look at that floor—old gum, dark splotches, sticky spots of unknown origin. Ugh. I can't even tolerate thinking about what microbial vermin are lurking there." She quivered in disgust.

"I've never heard of such a thing," said Boris. "I think you're making it up."

"It's a valid ailment," she said. "I have proof. A medical diagnosis, written by one of Pinnimuk City's most respected physicians. It's—uh—in my purse. Over there."

"Now what do we do?" asked Felicity, wringing her hands. She'd been patient, but now she was getting anxious. She had to get home.

"We wait," said the bus driver. "We wait until someone finds us."

Eighteen

On her drive home from school, Millicent thought about her desperate afternoon. Each tree-root crack in the sidewalk she drove over jolted a friend's face into her mind. *Thunk*. Juanita. Between classes, when Juanita saw Millicent coming down the hall, she had veered in another direction. *Thunk*. Pollock. In the library, Millicent tried to approach Pollock, who was sketching the Winifred T. Langley Memorial Fountain. He slammed his sketchbook shut and marched away. *Thunk*. Tonisha. Millicent had walked in on Tonisha applying her makeup in the girls' room. When Tonisha saw her, she immediately left with only one eye done. Millicent had been unable to get any of them to tolerate her long enough to hear her out.

I've got to find a way, she thought.

When Millicent reached her house, she went straight to the lab. She inserted her lab-door key, but it didn't fit in the lock. *That's weird.* She jogged around to the front door and went to the kitchen, where Uncle Phineas stood preparing tea.

"No doubt you tried the lab, yes?" he asked, not turning to face her.

"My key doesn't work."

"I thought to myself," said Uncle Phineas, pouring hot water into a mug, "what appropriate penalty could be served upon my dear, misguided niece?"

Millicent stopped and let her backpack drop to the floor. "Penalty? For what?"

Uncle Phineas turned toward her. "Despite my vow not to get involved in your private affairs, I unintentionally saw the formula for this creation you call Hooky Spray." He produced the notepaper on which Millicent had scribbled her formula for Hooky Spray and handed it to her. "Inventors must take care not to leave their secrets in plain view."

"Oh," she said, taking the paper. She'd forgotten she'd left the lab a mess, her notes strewn across a lab table.

"'Oh' is one word," he said. "So is 'unethical.' So is 'unprincipled.' So is '*wrong*.'"

Millicent felt her face tingle and her throat become tight.

"Yes, wrong," he continued. His features became stern, an out-of-the-ordinary expression for his otherwise cheerful face. "Inventors have a solemn duty to improve people's lives through their creativity and cunning. They do not make people's lives more uncomfortable. They do not give people phony illnesses. They do not clog people's noses. Yes?"

"I . . . can explain," Millicent said. Before she could stop herself, the events of the past two days began to spill from her mouth all mixed up and run together. "But first there was Tonisha and Fletch and I went to the principal's office because I was in the sink and before that Pollock and Juanita were mad at me and after that Pollywog had a love note written on his butt and I didn't know who to tell about the robbery and I sneezed really loud in English class and Tonisha isn't speaking to me and Roderick asked me out for pizza—yuck—and there's going to be a wedding and—" She grabbed the hem of his lab coat and bawled into it.

Uncle Phineas bent down and patted her head. "Sinks and robberies, pizza and sneezing and weddings—you've had quite a couple of days."

"I have," she agreed, sniffling.

He straightened himself. "However . . ."

Millicent's heart sank.

"As nail-biting as it all sounds, these mishaps are not sufficient to prohibit a punishment for inventing this concoction you call Hooky Spray."

"But—" Millicent groaned.

"I thought about it for a good, long while," he continued.

153

"As much as it pained me, I happened upon three ideas, a triumvirate of punishments, if you will. Number one: your access to the lab has been denied for a full week. This will afford you time to consider the import of what you invent in there. Number two: you are grounded—no after-school activities and no friends. Number three: you are to hand over this Hooky Spray immediately." He held out his palm.

Millicent plunged her hand in her pocket and paused. If she gave him the Hooky Spray, how would she keep the bullies from smelling Bully-Be-Gone? She eased the bottle from her pocket, handing it to him with a near-silent huff.

"I hate doing this, Millicent," Uncle Phineas said. "Truly."

She'd never been mad at Uncle Phineas before, but he'd become more unfair than she'd ever remembered him to be. Her blood curdled in her cheeks, growing hot with each mental tally of the punishments he'd lined up for her. How could he take away her favorite things? How could he not see that she'd only created the Hooky Spray to help her friends? She could almost feel steam jetting from her ears. Just as she opened her mouth to protest, she detected the faint aroma of her mother's blueberry scented Blue Be-Hairy Hair Spray and her father's Loco for Cocoa Shaving Cream. Memories of her parents ran slide-show fast through her brain. Her heart softened, her face slackened into a sloppy grin. Her hands, previously clenched, unwound like balls of yarn. She realized that, of course, Uncle Phineus was right to punish her; he always knew what was best. She really should listen to him more often and be more helpful—

Hey, wait a second! Her reaction bore a similarity to the result of smelling Bully-Be-Gone. She shook her head.

"That other creation," Uncle Phineas said, "the packet you left on the lab table. Now that's an invention with a nobler objective, though the plausibility of warding off bullies with cologne is dubious. Yes?"

He had tried Bully-Be-Gone! "Uh-huh," Millicent managed to squeak.

"Nevertheless, your goal was a decent one."

"Decent goal." Millicent nodded. "It—it . . ." she stuttered, trying to think of a way to find out if he'd had any extraordinary experiences lately.

"Doesn't do anything, I'm sorry to say," he answered.

"Yeah," she said, silently relieved.

"Besides, I don't know any bullies," he added, "unless you count that disagreeable clerk at the market downtown. She actually said good morning to me today and gave me the sappiest grin."

Millicent froze.

"Inexplicable," Uncle Phineas said. "Anyway, your punishments will now commence. To your room."

Millicent thought about begging for her freedom, but decided against it. She went upstairs, already thinking up a scheme to get her Hooky Spray back.

Nineteen

Two hours later, the sun was setting upon the bus passengers. The sky transformed into a yellow mass, brilliant as pollen. The clouds went poppy orange edged with rose-colored fringe. The whole sunset looked like the inside of some fantastic flower. Within the bus, however, the passengers were unappreciative of its beauty. They grew more and more anxious as the bear stalked around the bus; sometimes sitting, sometimes standing to smell the windows. Incredibly, they'd seen no cars pass by. To while away the wait and to ease their tensions, they told each other about themselves.

It turned out the man in the suit was named Mr. Wayfersson. He was a snack-and-cracker salesman. His briefcase was full of cracker and cookie samples—Nibblies, Chompies, and Gnaw-Do-Wells, to name a few—which he guarded nervously. Dallas Cheval, the cowboy, was on his way to Masonville's annual ropers' show. He even demonstrated his lasso skills, but very carefully, so as not to upset the balance of the bus. Clay and Cleon were expected at their aunt's house. Permitted by their mother to bring only one toy each, they'd chosen their slingshots. The librarian Miss Dewey was going to Masonville to help christen a new wing of the library. Anne had driven buses for forty years. If she ever had a question about retiring before, she'd become unquestionably sure she would "hang up her driving gloves" in the very near future and settle down in the plains, far from the mountains. Boris told them about his piggyback racing career.

By the time Felicity finished her own extraordinary tale, nightfall had come and the bear was napping against the bus in a furry heap.

"We're hungry," the twins whimpered.

"We all are," said Anne, "but there isn't any food—unless . . ." She raised her eyebrow at Mr. Wayfersson's briefcase.

"No way," he said, clutching the satchel to his chest. "These are my samples. I need them to sell my brand-new product line."

"We're starving," Dallas said.

"Yeah, we're starving," complained Boris.

Felicity knew hunger better than any of them, but she said nothing. They were being such big babies.

"No," growled Mr. Wayfersson.

"No?" asked Miss Dewey curtly. "Let me put it to you this way. We'll probably be eaten by a bear or go careening down a cliff. In either case, you'll be kissing your crackers good-bye soon."

Mr. Wayfersson thought about it. He sighed. "Tough logic to argue," he said at last, unlocking his briefcase. "Just open the wrappers carefully. Maybe I can sell them off the pretty packaging." He popped the lid of his brief-case, revealing an array of bright, cellophane-wrapped goodies. Cleon reached out to snatch a snack. "Ah, ah, ah!" exclaimed Mr. Wayfersson, raising his palm as if he were going to smack Cleon's hand. "Not so fast with those grubby little digits."

Cleon recoiled and started weeping. "I don't have g-g-g-grubby d-d-d-digits," he said. "What are grubby digits?"

"Dirty fingers," said Miss Dewey.

"Oh," said Cleon, sniffling and examining his finger-nails. "Okay. I have those."

Mr. Wayfersson swiveled the briefcase so that its open-ing faced him. He pushed his glasses farther up his nose. "Let's see," he said thoughtfully. "To whom shall I give which snack?"

"Does it matter?" snapped Boris.

"And who will go snackless?" Mr. Wayfersson responded.

"Aside from Nibblies, Chompies, and Gnaw-Do-Wells," he continued, "I have a wide assortment of delectables. There are Chocolate and Marshmallow Bunk Beds, 'Piled high for the mouth with little floor space'; Encyclopedia Saltines, 'A fun fact on every snack'; Pony Puffs, 'One herd is never enough'—"

"Must you run down the entire list? And who cares about the slogans?" huffed Boris. "My stomach is fluttery."

"I also have Auto Mall Crackers," said Mr. Wayfersson, paying no heed to Boris. "There's a little jingle to go with them," he added, then cleared his throat. "Auto Mall Crackers in my coupe," he sang, "diesels and sportscars loop the loop."

"Good heavens," said Boris, burying his head in his hands.

"Last, but not least, I have Pork Clouds, 'You'll give 'em up when pigs fly,' and a small box of Engagement Bagel Rings, 'One bite and you're committed.' See?" he asked, holding the box for them to view. "They have rock salt diamonds on them. Now, who shall get what? That's the question."

"Isn't it obvious?" shouted Boris, moving his rubber pig nose to his forehead with a snap of elastic.

"No," said Mr. Wayfersson, truly puzzled.

"For crying out loud. The Chocolate and Marshmallow Bunk Beds should go to the twins because they have small mouths and because twins often sleep in bunk beds. Am I not right?" Boris asked.

"You are right," Clay and Cleon said in unison. "We do have small mouths and sleep in bunk beds."

"There," Boris said smugly. "Furthermore, the Encyclopedia Saltines should go to Miss Dewey because she's a librarian. The Pony Puffs should go to Dallas because he's a cowboy. Anne should have the Auto Mall Crackers because she's a driver. You can pass the Pork Clouds to me because I am the very essence of porkness. And the Engagement Bagel Rings should go to Felicity because—well, look at her." Boris repositioned his pig nose over his real one. "Some salesman you are," he added.

"No need to get nasty," said Mr. Wayfersson, pursing his lips. With tremendous care, as if he were handling ancient relics, he passed the appropriate snack to the appropriate person and took for himself a Gnaw-Do-Well. Everyone, except Mr. Wayfersson, began to tear into the packets greedily. "Hey, hey, hey," he scolded. "Gently, please. I want the wrappers when you're done."

The passengers ate slowly, savoring each nibble as if they wouldn't ever see food again.

Life as a homeless person had taught Felicity to save food. She opened her box of Engagement Bagel Rings and automatically placed two inside her jacket pocket before consuming the bulk of them. Storing food in her pockets was a habit bound to stay with her for a while.

They were nearly finished when they felt a thump against the side of the bus. It was the bear again, aroused by the smell of snacks.

160

"Quick," said Anne, "stuff 'em in your traps."

Everyone did as advised, cramming the remaining food into their mouths. Then they sat there, in the indigo-blue night, their cheeks as bloated as squirrels' full of nuts, their eyes pale moons of terror. The bear harrumphed and sauntered around to the other side of the bus, sniffing, sniffing, sniffing. They chewed as fast as they could and swallowed.

They sat as still as trees, for as long as they were able to keep their eyes open, but eventually, one by one, as the night went from blue to black, they drifted off to sleep.

Twenty

Millicent listened at her bedroom wall, a drinking glass to her ear, waiting for the telltale sound of Uncle Phineas sleeping. She didn't have to wait long. Soon, his snoring reverberated through the wall. She went to his bedroom door and opened it as carefully as she could. The door creaked. Uncle Phineas snorted loudly as if he were saying Who's there? Millicent froze. A full minute passed before she was satisfied he wouldn't awaken. She tiptoed into his room.

In the corner, piled on a chair along with other clothing, she spied his lab coat. He'd kept it on all afternoon and, she'd noticed, he'd left the bottle of Hooky Spray in its pocket. She crept over to the coat. Uncle Phineas snorted again, a loud, walrusy sound that made her heart pound. With the stealth of a snake, her hand slid into the pocket of his coat and clasped the bottle of Hooky Spray.

A pang hit Millicent in the stomach. She looked at Uncle Phineas sleeping soundly and unaware of her misdeed. *I'm sorry*, she thought before gliding out of his room as silently as a breeze.

A short time later Millicent sat at her desk, under the warm glow of a desk lamp. She'd hooked up the lamp to her chair some time ago, so that when she sat down, her weight would light the lamp. *Keeping* the lamp lit was another problem altogether—she had to rock back and forth to keep it on.

She thought about the Hooky Spray.

How was she going to get close to the bullies? She decided she would catch them first thing in the morning at the bike racks, where they'd be locking their bicycles. While she was there, she'd be able to check their bikes to see if they were indeed from the Mega-Stupenda Mart as she suspected. If her assumptions proved correct, she would tell Juanita, whose father, Officer Romero Alonso, was a policeman. She could spray the bullies and send them to jail at the same time. It felt like a plan, until she remembered that Juanita wasn't speaking to her.

Just then, her phone rang, startling her out of her chair

and causing the lamp to turn off. She picked up the receiver promptly so that Uncle Phineas wouldn't wake up. It was ten o'clock and he'd already been asleep for an hour. She turned the ringer volume as low as it could go.

"Millicent?"

She recognized the voice on the other end of the line as Roderick's. She rummaged through her desk drawer for a hanky. She found one and put it over the mouthpiece. Lowering her voice as much as possible, she answered. "Uh, Millicent's not here," she said, sitting down.

"Who is this?" asked Roderick.

"A very old friend of the family," she said.

"Well, could you tell Millicent that Roderick called?" he asked.

"Uh, sure. Bye-bye," she said.

"And that I'd still like to go out for pizza with her," he said.

"Gross," she squealed, then lowered her voice. "I mean, okay. Bye-bye."

"And that I miss her?" asked Roderick.

"Blechhh," said Millicent. "I mean, okay. Bye-bye."

"And that—" Roderick said.

Millicent hung up before he had the chance to finish. Her desk light was still off because she wasn't rocking.

The phone rang again. She padded the mouthpiece with the hanky, assuming it was Roderick.

"Hello?" she said in her deepest voice.

"Is Millicent there?" It was Tonisha.

"Oh," said Millicent, removing the hanky. "It's me."

"Humph," Tonisha grunted. "I'm calling to tell you to keep away from Fletchie."

"Oh, oh, oh," Millicent muttered, "I, uh, I, uh, I, uh." Millicent felt suddenly nauseous. "I have to tell you something."

"You have nothing to tell me," Tonisha shouted.

"B-b-but—" stammered Millicent.

"But nada," said Tonisha. "Do me a favor: stay away from me—from all of us. I don't even want to see you at the extravaganza tomorrow."

A sharp beep pierced Millicent's eardrum. She had another call coming in.

"Wait, wait," she said. "Tonisha, there's a call on the other line. Please don't hang up."

She clicked over to the second line.

"Hello?" she said, her voice high and squeaky.

"Is that you, Millicent, honey?" asked Roderick.

"Yuck!" she screeched.

She plucked up the hanky and jammed it onto the mouthpiece.

"No," she said in a mannish tone. "Millicent isn't back yet."

"It's Roderick. Can you tell her I called?" he asked.

"Glad to, glad to," she said. "Gotta go."

She clicked back to the main line, hoping to explain it all to Tonisha, but she'd hung up.

Twenty-one

Morning light came slicing between the mountain peaks, beaming laserlike onto the faces of the passengers. Clay and Cleon were the first to awaken. Rubbing their eyes, then stretching, they whispered to each other.

"Is it still there?" asked Clay.

"I don't know," Cleon replied.

They stood up on the seat and peeked out the window. The bear was asleep against the left rear tire.

"I wish I had a rock," said Clay.

"I'd shoot it," said his brother.

"That would only aggravate it," said Felicity, rubbing

the sleep out of her eyes and staring out the window.

"What will we do, then?" Clay asked.

"I intend to figure that out." Felicity was already in deep concentration, staring out the window. "Let me see one of those slingshots."

Cleon handed her his. "They shoot stuff really far," he said. "Far, far, far. I once shot a hard-boiled egg across our yard and our neighbor's yard and our neighbor's neighbor's yard."

"Yeah," said Clay. "I once shot a chicken drumstick across the street into an open mailbox. You shoulda' seen the neighbor's dog chase it and jump up and down trying to get at it. So funny." He shook his head and flapped his arms, imitating the bumbling leaping of the dog.

Felicity wasn't amused. "I'm sure you've been told this, but you shouldn't play with your food," she said. Given her experience living without a home or the luxury of regular meals, she found the wasting of food unforgivable. She examined the slingshot and tugged on the rubber strap. *Food is a precious necessity and taken for granted by most folks.* She snapped the rubber strap. *Food should not replace toys for entertainment and it should not, without a doubt, be shot with a slingshot.* She pretended to aim the slingshot. *Much less, food should not be used to make an animal run clear across a busy street where— That's it!* "Never mind my previous comment. You've given me an idea," she said. "Let's wake everyone."

When the other passengers were all awake and over the

initial, hazy-minded realization that they were still on a bus, on a cliff, with a bear outside, Felicity put her scheme into action.

"Mr. Wayfersson," she said, "of the snacks you have left, which is your heaviest and smelliest?"

"Excuse me?" he asked. "I take offense at the implication I have smelly snacks."

"Most fragrant," Felicity corrected. "Which of your snacks is most fragrant?"

"Let me look," he said, lifting his briefcase. He rummaged in it for a minute. "I suppose the Swiss Cheese Moon Rocks would qualify for both the heaviest and most aromatic categories."

"You didn't tell us you had Swiss Cheese Moon Rocks," grumbled Boris.

"They were discontinued," replied Mr. Wayfersson. "Too hard."

"But perfect for my plan to get us out of this mess," said Felicity.

She went on to explain her ingenious idea. Clay and Cleon would lure the bear away from the bus by shooting one Moon Rock at a time farther and farther up the road through the emergency roof hatch. The bear, being dependent on its sense of smell, would be enticed by the cheese snacks and would, Felicity surmised, follow its nose. Clay and Cleon would carry on discharging Moon Rocks until the bear was at a safe enough distance that the bus occupants could climb through the bus's emergency exit and make a run for it. Felicity waited for everyone's response, smiling so hard her cheeks tingled.

"Risky, but I think it will work," said Miss Dewey.

"I think so, too," Anne said. "How exciting."

"Hot dang, little lady," said Dallas. "You're a smart one!"

"Thank you," Felicity said, her eyes bright.

"There's one huge problem," said Boris in a somber yet simpering tone. "Let's say the twins are able to coax the bear to a reasonable distance from the bus. And let's just say we are graced with enough time to leave the bus. Has it crossed your mind that, with every person who exits, the bus will grow lighter and lighter? Have you considered the inevitability of the bus falling hundreds of feet to the valley below? Did it occur to you that some of us will not make it to freedom—that, instead, you would be sending some of us to certain death? And what criteria, pray tell, would you use to determine who shall live and who shall perish? Did any of this enter your noggin?" He tapped his temple with his forefinger, sneering at her triumphantly.

Felicity's happy expression sunk into a dismal pout.

"I didn't think so, Miss Hot-Dang Smartypants," he said.

"There must be something we can do," whispered Felicity, on the verge of tears. She had to make it home. She was so close, so very close. Visions of her husband's handsome face sailed across her mind, powered by a wind of memory. By now, he surely looked different. *Time has a way of doing that to people,* she thought. He probably had fragile lines on his face, like fine, cracked china. Maybe his hair was gone, maybe not. But she would still love him because she had never stopped, despite her memory loss. She had to make it home.

She looked out the window while everyone talked. Behind the bus, across the two-lane highway, was a boulder. Its base, as big around as a small house, rose ten feet to a hooked tip. She studied it, almost absentmindedly, her eyes sparkling with tears. Then she was struck with another brilliant idea.

"Dallas, can you rope something bigger than a bull?"

"Sure," said Dallas. "Why?"

Felicity beamed, clasped her hands together, and said, "Here's what we're going to do. . . ."

Dallas was tall enough to push open the trapdoor in the roof and tall enough to stick his head out, but not his torso.

"I need to sit on someone's shoulders," he called quietly to the others, careful not to wake the bear.

Everyone looked at Boris.

"Don't look at me," he said.

"But you're a professional piggyback racer," Miss Dewey said. "You make a living carrying people on your back."

"Perhaps he's a fake," Felicity said in a cool voice.

"I am not," growled Boris.

"Why did you say you had a bad back?" asked Felicity.

"I said no such thing," Boris answered hotly.

"You did so. When we were scrambling to the back of the bus. *I have a bad back*," she said, imitating his sniveling tone. Boris's eyebrows quivered. "And you're afraid of speed," Felicity continued, remembering how inconsistent he seemed to her when they'd met. The pieces were falling into place. "And your uniform doesn't fit you. It appears to have been tailored for someone else. *And* you don't have any publicity photos. Why, I don't think you're a real piggyback racer at all."

Boris glanced out a window. "I am, too," he said softly.

"What are you, really?" asked Felicity.

Boris was silent. He bit his lower lip and twiddled his thumbs. "Promise you won't laugh?" he finally asked.

"Promise," they all replied.

"I'm a shoe changer," he said so quietly they couldn't hear him.

"A what?" asked Felicity, cupping her ear.

"A shoe changer," Boris said, a little louder this time.

"A shoe changer?" reiterated Felicity.

"Yes. I work in the pit. During a race, when piggyback racers need a change of shoes, they pull over and I unlace their racing boots and put new ones on them."

An uncomfortable quiet filled the bus.

"That's a very nice job to have," Felicity said, suddenly sorry she'd exposed him.

"I wanted to be a piggyback racer," Boris said, sitting down and resting his elbow on his knee and his chin on his upturned palm. "I trained and trained, running the track with an actual-sized dummy on me. I was so close to becoming a pro, but instead of strengthening me, the rigorous training gave me a herniated disk." He went on to explain that, because of the bad back he'd gotten from training, he was unable to carry a rider and was therefore withdrawn from racing contention. Because of his injury, he was forced to give up his dream of piggyback racing glory and was hired on as a member of the pit crew. "The truth is," he concluded sadly, "I'm a fraud. I'm not famous at all."

"Unfulfilled dreams tend to make a person bitter," said Miss Dewey. "I read that someplace."

"Miss Dewey, not now," scolded Felicity. She sat down next to Boris, her wedding dress enveloping the two of them in their own confidential cloud. "As a human cannonball, I was famous," she said to him gently. "It's not a big deal."

For the first time on the trip, Boris smiled a real smile. "Truly?" he asked.

"Absolutely," Felicity answered. "You have no privacy, reporters go through your garbage searching for publishable tidbits of your personal life, and having a peaceful dinner out is unthinkable."

Boris seemed to be contemplating her observation. "Nevertheless, I'd like to be famous, if only for fifteen minutes," he said.

"Well, if you truly want it, it can happen," Felicity commented.

"So, is someone going to help me or not?" asked Dallas, his head still sticking out of the trapdoor.

At Anne's urging, they all pitched in, with the exception of the twins who stood in wait for their part in the plan. The adults created a platform of their linked arms: hand to wrist, hand to wrist. Dallas hoisted himself onto their makeshift scaffold, clutching his lasso and apologizing for his pointy boots.

"I see the boulder," he said to the people below.

There was a whooshing of rope. Felicity watched the looped end of the lasso glide through the air and neatly catch on the boulder.

"He got it," she said, trying to keep her voice down.

They cheered as quietly as they could, then eased Dallas down until he was able to stand. "That was easy," he said.

"Twins," Felicity whispered, "are you ready?"

"Yes, ma'am," they replied.

"Cheesy nuggets?" Felicity asked.

"They're called Swiss Cheese Moon Rocks," said Mr. Wayfersson, handing the twins a fistful of the hard, pungent biscuits.

"Whatever," said Felicity.

While the twins were being elevated, Dallas tied the other end of his rope to the legs of two bus seats in a complex series of knots, completing his part in Felicity's plan. The seats were bolted to the floor and Felicity thought this would be a secure enough anchor to keep the bus from going over the cliff. At least it would be secure enough for them to make a neat, fast escape—she hoped.

"It's still asleep," Cleon called down.

"Cleon and Clay," Felicity said, "you must never, ever, ever, ever again do what I am about to ask you to do—to any animal at any time in your futures. Promise?"

"We promise," they replied.

"Swear?"

"We swear."

"Good," Felicity said. She cleared her throat. "I want you to aim for the bear's head."

"What?" they asked.

"That's not nice," said Clay.

"I think our mom would be mad if she found out," said Cleon. "We could get into trouble."

"I know, I know," Felicity agreed. "But your mother won't find out, number one. Number two, we are in much more serious trouble presently. In predicaments such as ours, rules can be suspended. Safety, in this case, supersedes decorum."

"Huh?" they asked.

Miss Dewey piped up. "In other words, this time, it's okay to be slightly naughty to save our lives."

"Grown-ups are confusing," mumbled Clay to his brother.

"Yeah," said Cleon. "Do this, don't do that, do what I told you not to do and never do it again."

"Yeah," whispered Clay, "I guess getting older means getting dumber."

"Promise you won't tell our mom?" they asked in unison.

"We promise," said Felicity.

The twins popped their heads out the trapdoor. Lying on its back, snoring, was the bear. With every exhale, its lips looked like two fluttering pieces of bologna. Clay, who was the better aim of the two, poised his slingshot and loaded it with a Swiss Cheese Moon Rock.

"Not too hard," said Felicity.

Clay let the Moon Rock fly. It hit the bear square on the nose, then bounced off, landing a few feet away. With a roar, the bear shuddered awake.

Twenty-two

It was seven A.M. and Millicent hadn't slept at all. It wasn't for lack of trying, but whenever she closed her eyes, images of her angry friends entered her half-awake dreams.

She'd called Pollock the night before, after Tonisha had hung up on her. Pollock hung up, too, as soon as he heard her voice. She called Juanita—same response. She hadn't been able to keep anyone on the phone long enough to blurt out a warning. She spent the rest of the evening and into the morning devising and revising numerous strategies to end Bully-Be-Gone's chain of horrific events.

She stumbled out of bed to shower, her legs an uncooperative pair of noodles. Bleary-eyed and tired, she ran into the doorjamb on her way into the bathroom.

"How am I going to make it through today?" she asked herself.

Millicent wasn't a regular coffee drinker because a misinformed adult once told her that coffee stunted one's growth. She was a preschooler then. Now, she was older and had scientific evidence to the contrary. She showered and dressed, then tiptoed past Uncle Phineas's door. She had to get out of the house before he woke up and found the Hooky Spray missing.

Once downstairs, she made herself a cup of Lid-Yanker Morning Blend. On the package it said it was guaranteed to pull your eyelids back over your eyeballs with a single sip. She hoped it was true. She took a big gulp. Sure enough, her eyelids snapped open. She was as awake as she could hope to be.

"Wow." She picked up a spoon and examined her reflection on its convex side. She looked like a lemur.

Bristling with energy and sporting bugging eyeballs to match, she bounded upstairs. She emptied the contents of her backpack onto the floor, placing only the bottle of Hooky Spray inside. She donned a zip-front, hooded sweatshirt, swung a crocheted scarf around her neck, and was ready to go. Before she left, she placed a note on the kitchen counter that simply read: *Dear Uncle Phineas, I'm sorry. Love, Millicent.*

Throughout the morning, Millicent alternately felt like a fugitive, a hunter, and an outcast. First, she snuck out of the house after being grounded by Uncle Phineas. Half expecting him to appear around each corner, she skulked through school as nervous and twitchy as a criminal. Second, she had to get close enough to the bullies to squirt them with Hooky Spray, but she hadn't seen them all morning and had no idea where to find them. Third, her friends weren't speaking to her.

At lunch, she sat at the Wunderkind table in the cafeteria, spreading her lunch out in an inviting display, hoping her friends would join her. Pollock and Juanita showed up, chatting with each other, but when they saw Millicent they stopped talking except to say, "Let's sit at that table over there today."

Millicent called out, "I have something important to tell you." They ignored her, traipsing past as if she didn't exist. *Fine*, she thought. *They'll be thanking me once I stop the bullies from stalking them. I can wait.*

She put her lunch in her backpack and took it to the Winifred T. Langley Memorial Fountain. "Hi, Winifred," she said as she sat. "Gee. You're not talking to me either." She smiled at her joke—her only smile of the morning—and proceeded to eat her lunch alone.

Moments later, Tonisha walked by, scribbling a poem in her notepad. "Tonisha," Millicent said, setting her sandwich down. "Please—"

Tonisha muttered to herself, "Did you hear something?

I didn't hear anything," and kept going.

The end-of-lunch bell rang. Millicent rose to go to class when Roderick's voice startled her.

"Hi, honey," he said.

She spun around to face him. "Hi?" she asked more than stated.

"I've been looking for you," he said.

Of all the luck, Millicent thought, *the one person speaking to me is . . . him.* "You found me," she said. "Now I've got to go." She started for her next class, social science, at a brisk pace. Roderick kept pace with her, his fists pumping as if he were jogging.

"What about pizza? Have you thought about having pizza with me? Huh? Pizza? Gosh, you smell good," he panted.

Rounding a corner into the hallway, Millicent blurted, "I don't eat anymore."

"But you just had lunch."

"My last meal. Gotta lose weight."

"You're perfect the way you are."

Millicent bolted, dodging students as she raced for her classroom.

"You're perfect!" Roderick shouted. "Don't forget—pizza!"

Halfway through social science class Mr. Pennystacker made an announcement over the P.A. system. "All students participating in the Masonville Young Talent Extravaganza, please report to the Winifred T. Langley

Memorial Fountain in the next ten minutes. Your shuttle bus is waiting. Best of luck to you."

Millicent looked up from her social science book to glance out the window. To her surprise, Fletch snuck past, wearing an ill-fitting light-blue tuxedo. He darted from shrub to bush like a spy. Next, Pollywog lumbered past the window with only a small measure of Fletch's stealth. He wore a burgundy and gold brocade tuxedo that seemed to be straining to stay on him. Nina came last, scampering from one bush to another, as if she were playing hide-and-seek. She wore an ungainly wedding dress that was too long for her—except for the sleeves, which fit fine. She tripped on the hem of the dress and disappeared from view. Pollywog helped her up. She hit him and he fell into a bush.

"I have to take care of this before it's too late," Millicent said, unconscious she'd spoken aloud.

Mr. Kulcher, her social science teacher, stopped writing on the blackboard, nearly dropping his chalk. "Take care of what?"

"My—my—" She glanced at a photo of Albert Einstein Mr. Kulcher had taped to the chalkboard, her eyes landing on his full shiny forehead. To her, it looked like a . . . "Blister!" she said. "I have a huge blister—on my foot."

"That's disgusting," the girl in front of her said.

"Go to the school nurse," Mr. Kulcher said. "Skip the hall pass."

Millicent hobbled to the door. Once she was out of Mr. Kulcher's sight, she charged straight for her car.

Twenty-three

The bear roared again, angry at having been so painfully awakened. It heaved its bulk onto its four limbs and looked as if it might rip right through the side of the bus, it was so enraged. The passengers in the bus gasped and held their breaths. But then the bear's nose jiggled like a bonbon on a candy factory conveyor belt. It sniffed to the left and to the right.

The Swiss Cheese Moon Rock had landed several feet away from the bear's head after bouncing off its snout. Skimming its face along the road, the bear found the snack and gobbled it up.

"Another," Felicity urged, "farther away, Clay."

Clay aimed a few feet up the road and shot another one. The bear located that one as well. Clay kept shooting Swiss Cheese Moon Rocks until the bear was about twenty yards away, then he switched places with Cleon, who could shoot farther. Cleon coaxed the bear another twenty yards when they ran out of Swiss Cheese Moon Rocks.

"All gone," said Clay, climbing down Dallas's back.

The bear squatted in the distance, looking like nothing more than a mound of unraveled black yarn, sniffing for more snacks.

"Seems it's now or never," said Dallas, reaching for the hole in the roof.

They had decided that Dallas would be the first through the trapdoor since he was the strongest and would be able to lift everyone else out. However, he was also the heaviest. With much grunting, they all pitched in, pushing Dallas as best they could through the opening.

"Ow," Boris complained as the tip of Dallas's cowboy boot lodged itself in his ear. "Watch the boot, please."

Dallas's other foot flailed as he tried to hoist himself onto the bus roof. It found a foothold on Mr. Wayfersson's head.

"Hey!" whined Mr. Wayfersson. His hair slid down his forehead. He struggled to keep it in place.

"Toupee, eh?" asked Boris, voicing a question to which the answer was obvious. "Glad to see I'm not the only fake around here."

Dallas's legs disappeared through the trapdoor. His head popped through a second later.

"All righty," he said, adjusting his hat, "who's next?"

Felicity was next, they agreed, since she was the oldest of the group. Dallas drew her through the hole in a flash of white tulle. One by one, he easily lifted the rest of them as if they were babies out of the bus and onto the roof.

Now situated safely on top of the bus, they conferred in hushed voices, sporadically glancing at the bear. Its face was still to the ground, prowling for more food.

From that point on, their lives would depend on speed. Once again, Dallas would be first. He'd leap off the bus and help the others down as quickly as possible. Felicity volunteered to be last because she wanted to make sure everyone got off safely. The entire scheme was of her design, so she felt a motherly sort of obligation that the whole thing go according to plan. Everyone agreed to let her go last, but only if she hurried. They had calculated that, even though the bus was tied to a rock, it was merely a matter of time before the rope snapped and the bus hurtled into the valley below. When they hit the ground, they would all have to make a run for it, down the mountain road and away from the bear until they reached Masonville.

"Ready?" asked Dallas.

"As we'll ever be," said Mr. Wayfersson, buttoning up his blazer, straightening his tie, and pressing his toupee to his scalp.

Miss Dewey cleared her throat and in a quivering voice said, "If we don't make it, I'd just like to say that I enjoyed our—"

"Foolishness," huffed Anne. "We will make it."

"Got no choice," said Dallas, nodding. With that, he scooted on his bottom toward the edge of the roof and jumped off the bus. He landed with a loud thud.

In the distance, the blind bear's ears pricked up like two little satellite dishes, but it didn't turn toward the bus.

Dallas stood bracing himself to catch Clay and Cleon. They insisted on jumping together; so they did, hand in hand. Dallas caught them as easily as he would have two five-pound sacks of sugar.

To Miss Dewey, the roof of the bus was infinitely dirtier than its floor. From her skirt pocket, she removed a solitary tissue and began scouring a path in the caked-on soil as she crawled to the edge of the roof, whimpering.

"What in the blazes?" asked Boris.

"You leave me be, pork man," she said. "You leave me be." She scrubbed and crawled and scrubbed and crawled, muttering, until she found herself at the roof's edge. She stood and discarded the tissue.

"Uuuuummm," said Clay and Cleon. "She littered."

Dallas clamped their mouths shut with his hands.

"Oh, my," Miss Dewey sighed, fanning herself. "I made it. I don't know whether to laugh or cry."

"I don't know whether to push her or shove her," Boris said under his breath.

"Boris," scolded Felicity.

Finally, Miss Dewey jumped daintily into Dallas's arms.

Next, Anne dismounted the roof with little more than a grunt. Mr. Wayfersson came after, tossing his briefcase down first.

Boris walked to the edge of the roof.

"I'd better not get hurt," he hissed to Dallas. "You ready?"

"Yes, sir," Dallas answered.

"You sure?"

"Yup."

"I've got a bad back," said Boris. "Don't you forget it."

"How could we forget?" asked Felicity. "Just jump."

Dallas braced himself for Boris's impact.

Helter-skelter and arms flailing, Boris sailed into Dallas's arms. Dallas staggered a bit, regained his balance, and set Boris on the ground.

Felicity stood alone on top of the bus, the morning breeze raising her veil, making it flutter like a circus banner. She was finally going home. One jump and she'd be on her way. She turned, looking up the highway for the bear. It wasn't there. Last she saw it, it was about a hundred yards away. She scanned the road. Suddenly, she saw a black blur approaching the far corner of the bus.

"Run!" She screamed.

The bus started creaking. The group let out a collective gasp when they saw the rope pulled tight. They let out another collective gasp when they saw the bear. They seemed confused as to whether they should escape or wait for Felicity.

"Run," she screamed again.

"Not without you, little lady," said Dallas. "Hurry!" He held out his arms.

Felicity was about to leap when the wind kicked up, wrapping her skirt around her uplifted leg, blowing her veil into her face. She lost her footing and fell off the bus. Dallas did his best to catch her, but he fell, too, leaving them both in a tangled heap of netting and denim. Dallas popped up and lifted Felicity onto her feet.

The bear sniffed and growled just a few yards away.

"Oh, oh, oh," Felicity groaned, buckling over in pain. "I twisted my ankle. I can't stand on it."

"Rats," Boris said gruffly. "The rest of you run. I'll take it from here."

They stood, frozen.

"Run," Boris yelled, waving them off.

They started to run, glancing over their shoulders, their faces imprinted with worry.

"Get on my back," said Boris.

"What?" asked Felicity.

"Good heavens," said Boris. "Doesn't anyone around here do as they're told? I said get on my blasted back."

"But—"

"Now!" yelled Boris.

Felicity climbed onto his back, fitted her arms into his

padded piggyback racer harness, and clamped her legs around his waist.

Boris took off in a chorus of squeaking leather. And just in time. There was a sharp twang as the rope snapped in two, and the bus, screeching and scraping, went over the cliff into the valley below. The bear bellowed loudly, alarmed at the sound of the bus and at having lost its eight-course breakfast.

"**A**aaawwww, gaaaawd," screeched Boris. "Such pain." He galloped along, Felicity on his back, whining and moaning.

"Really, Boris," said Felicity. "Put me down. I'll try to manage myself."

"No, no. Quite all right," he said. "Aaaawwww, gaaaawd. Torment! Misery! Agony!"

"I think I can at least walk," Felicity assured him.

"No, no. Won't hear of it," he said. "Oh, help me! Daggers of anguish in my back!"

"Please, Boris, put me down," said Felicity. She wasn't sure what was worse—being eaten by a bear or suffering Boris's whining.

"No, no. No can do," he said. "Aaaawwww, gaaaawd. My tortured, bedeviled spine!"

On it went, Boris's howling and Felicity's pleading, as they made their way down the final Curmudgeonly Mountain. Their traveling companions were several paces ahead of them, their hands protecting their ears from

Boris's grating voice as they ran. They'd put a good length between the bear and themselves. In fact, they couldn't see it anymore. Nevertheless, they kept a fast pace.

Soon, they reached an intersection on the crest of a small hill. To their left, a road slithered its way up the hill slightly and into the forest. Below, they could see Masonville stretching out like a blanket, the glistening green bay just beyond.

"Rest," called Anne to the others. "Let's catch our breaths."

Everyone came to a halt with Boris and Felicity bringing up the rear.

"Which way?" asked Dallas.

Felicity was happy that she remembered the intersection. When she was a child, her family went on many outings to the woods around here. "The road to the left goes into Curmudgeonly State Park; the one we're on goes to Masonville." The road bent dramatically, then unfurled downhill like a hair ribbon.

"Then this is our road," said Dallas.

"Oh, oh, oh," panted Boris, shifting his weight. "Aaaawwww, gaaaawd. The sheer pain of it all."

A sportscar came buzzing up the highway ahead of them, a young man at the wheel, a young woman in the passenger seat.

"We must warn them," said Anne, stepping into the highway. She waved the car to a halt.

The man stared at the group before saying, "Good

morning. What are you all doing out on the road so early? I rarely see people here at this hour."

"We've had a near run-in with a ravenous bear about a mile farther up the road," Anne informed the driver.

"How frightening!" exclaimed the female passenger.

"Are you and your friends okay?" the man asked.

"Yes," Anne replied, "but you should turn around."

"Right. We don't want a brush with a bear, do we?" the man asked her friend, who shook her head worriedly. "I'm sorry we can't offer all of you a ride into town," he added, indicating with a bob of his head that his auto could accommodate only two people.

"We'll be fine," Anne said, patting the hood of his car.

Felicity was about to ask if the driver could at least take Clay and Cleon with them when the man made a Y-turn and rolled back toward town.

Twenty-four

On her way to Lulu Davinsky's Diamond Theater, Millicent came to an intersection near the edge of town where she saw what she first thought was the makings of a strange parade coming toward her. Running down the street was a cowboy in jeans, a plaid shirt, and a ten-gallon hat. Behind him was a tall, slender, studious-looking woman in a periwinkle-blue floral-print dress. Following close was a man in a suit, holding a briefcase close to his chest. Next came a woman in a gray uniform, holding the hands of two boys—twins it seemed. But the most bizarre members of the troupe trailed farther behind. A man in a pink leather suit, wincing and whining, was carrying a very old bride, in an orange parka, on his back.

Millicent sat, dumbfounded, watching as they tramped toward her. One by one they passed and waved. Millicent waved back.

"Whoa," said the old bride as the pink leather man approached Millicent's car.

"Okay," said the pink leather man, slowing to a walking pace. "Aaaawwww gaaawwwwd. Big ugly pain!"

Millicent saw that the man wore a rubber pig nose on his face and advertisements for breakfast meats on his outfit.

"Excuse me, miss," said the old bride. "Can you tell me if the police department is still located in the town square?"

"Well, y-y-yes," stammered Millicent. "Yes, it is."

Millicent thought there was something very familiar about the old bride—as if she'd seen her in a picture somewhere.

"Very good. Thank you," replied the woman. "Onward, Boris," she said to the pink leather man.

He trotted off, crying, "Aaaawwww, gaaaawwwwd. Terrible bayonets of affliction stabbing my back!"

Slightly stunned, Millicent turned to watch them hasten toward the town square. "If that isn't the weirdest thing I've ever seen, I don't know what is," she said to herself.

By the time Millicent pulled up to the theater, people were gathered outside, waiting for the doors to open.

She parked her car on the sidewalk and scanned the crowd for Tonisha, Pollock, and Juanita.

Lulu Davinsky's Diamond Theater was one of the oldest masonry buildings in Masonville. For the Masonville Young Talent Extravaganza, it had been decorated with yards and yards of streamers, printed to look like bricks. Masonville, after all, took pride in its reputation as Home of the Really Big Brick. Almost every special town event required some sort of reference to bricks. The Big Brick itself sat in front of the Diamond Theater in a circular brick planter frothing over with chrysanthemums, on a plinth made of bricks. The Extravaganza Committee had embellished the Big Brick with cardboard letters that read, "Extrava" on one side and "Ganza," on the other—because, while the brick was big, it wasn't quite big enough.

Millicent got out of her car and patted her sweatshirt pocket to make sure she had the Hooky Spray. Relieved to find that it hadn't fallen out, she plunged into the crowd to scout for her friends and the bullies, whom she figured would be close by. A few minutes of searching produced no results so she made her way around the corner to the stage door.

Leaning against the building, close to the stage door, were three bikes, sporting signs that read JUST MARRIED. Attached to the rear of each bike were strings with tin cans tied to them.

"Ugh," Millicent grunted. But now, she finally had her opportunity to search the bikes for evidence they were from the Mega-Stupenda Mart. She got closer to the bicycles to examine them. It took only a second to find the signature red and yellow Mega-Stupenda Mart price stickers. "Aha," she said. "Just as I thought. Leave it to the three of them to forget to take the tags off their stolen goods." Millicent steeled herself. Now, she not only had to stop the bullies from ruining the extravaganza for her friends, she also had to find a way to bring them to justice.

The stage door was propped open. Near it, a girl in a sequined leotard practiced twirling her flaming baton while roller-skating backward in circles. "Excuse me," Millicent said, darting into the theater.

The lights were dimmed backstage. Most of the contestants must have been already seated out front. Millicent could make out the shapes of some props set up in the wings. She heard voices coming from behind the heavy red velvet drapes. "If you want them back," she heard Nina say, "you'll have to marry us."

Want what back? Millicent snuck around the puddle of curtains, making certain she remained in the shadows.

Nina, Fletch, and Pollywog stood with their backs to the closed curtains, right in the center of the stage where the drapes would part. Nina gripped Pollock's portfolio with both of her spidery hands. Fletch held Tonisha's poetry notebook, and Pollywog hugged Juanita's violin case, smooching its neck.

"You give those back, now!" Pollock demanded.

Nina removed a painting from Pollock's portfolio and a

key from her pocket. She pointed the key at the canvas as if it were a knife.

"No," Pollock said.

"No? Is that your answer to my proposal?" Nina asked, pressing the key into the canvas.

"Stop it, Nina," Tonisha said. "Fletchie, why don't you do something about this?"

"I've proposed, too," Fletch said, "and you haven't answered." He opened her book of poetry and threatened to rip a page out, grasping it between his thumb and forefinger.

"Me, too," Pollywog said, removing Juanita's violin from its case. Juanita squealed in horror.

Millicent bit her lower lip. The extravaganza would be starting in less than three minutes. If the bullies destroyed her friends' most prized possessions, Juanita, Tonisha, and Pollock would be disqualified from the competition and they'd surely never speak to her again. But what could she do? How could she get close enough to the bullies to squirt them with Hooky Spray?

"If you so much as call for help," Nina said, "the violin, the book, and the paintings are goners. So what's it gonna be? Marriage or . . ." She pressed the key into Pollock's painting until it dimpled. Fletch tore an inch into a page of Tonisha's poetry, and Pollywog pulled on a string on Juanita's violin.

Suddenly a voice boomed over the sound system. "Welcome, ladies and gentlemen, to the Masonville Young

Talent Extravaganza." Millicent could hear applause from the other side of the curtain.

"You can still compete," Nina said. "All we need is a yes."

"We can be joined in holy mattress money," Pollywog said to Juanita.

"It's matrimony, dummy," Juanita said. "And give me my violin."

"I can't believe you're doing this, Fletch," Tonisha said, her eyes tearing up.

"When this is over," Millicent whispered to herself, "I'm giving up inventing for good."

She rushed onstage into the bright lights. Millicent had never been on a stage before or in front of a large audience. The shock of it winded her for a second—all those faces staring at her.

"Seems it's our first act in the vocal division," the emcee said, looking at his list of performers.

"Vocal?" Millicent asked.

"Miss Iva Asimova singing 'Let Me Call You Sweetheart,'" the emcee continued, "in her native Czech."

"Czech?" Millicent shrieked, shooting the emcee a glare.

The audience applauded warmly.

Millicent approached the microphone stand and tapped the mic—*thump, thump, thump*. "Oh. Microphone is on," she said in her best and only Czech accent. "Is good." She put one hand in her sweatshirt pocket and grabbed the microphone with the other. "Um. In my homeland, love is, how you say, like new bread from oven." She inched backward toward the curtain. "Is warm and smells good." She backed up a little more. Suddenly, the orchestra struck the first note of the song. "Oh. But if you eat too soon, is hot like . . . how you say . . . oven coils. Will burn your lips on good-smelling bread." The orchestra went into the song. "Oh. Song is coming." She backed all the way into the curtain. The orchestra got to the part where she was supposed to start singing, holding the note, waiting for her to join in. "Is my cue," she said. "Vet-ne-vall-nu-schveeeee-naaaaacht!" she sang as she took the bottle of Hooky Spray from her pocket. Reaching behind her, she stuck her arm in the separation between the curtain panels and sprayed, not once but several squirts, up and down and around and around.

Someone in the audience booed. "She's awful," someone else shouted. "Get her off the stage!"

Several huge sneezes exploded from backstage, bringing the orchestra to an abrupt halt.

Unsure of what to do next, Millicent nervously scanned the audience until her gaze landed on Officer Romero Alonso, Juanita's father. In a flash, a plan came to her. She looked to her right at a stagehand who stood gripping the curtain cord. "Please to open curtains for big finale," she said. "Then please to turn off footlights." The stagehand did as instructed, pulling on the cord until the red velvet drapes skidded apart. Then he went to the light board and turned off the footlights.

Backlit only by the spotlights upstage, Nina's, Fletch's, and Pollywog's silhouettes—long-armed, tall, and round— looked like black construction-paper cutouts on a white sheet.

Pollock, Tonisha, and Juanita grabbed their things from the bullies and ran offstage.

Juanita's father, Officer Romero Alonso, leaped from his seat. "The Mega-Stupenda Mart bike bandits!" he shouted and was out of his chair, bounding toward the stage, hand-cuffs at the ready.

"You're a hero, Millicent," said Officer Romero Alonso, as his partner, Herb, escorted Nina, Fletch, and Pollywog into their squad car. "You single-handedly cap-tured the notorious Mega-Stupenda Mart bike bandits. And incognito, to boot, posing as a contestant. Iva Asimova. That's a good one. How did you ever devise that scheme? That was clever."

"Believe me," she answered, "there was no cleverness involved."

"But you must be clever. You're the inventor of the spray that incapacitated the thieves, aren't you?" he asked.

"I *was* the inventor," she said, examining her finger-nails. "I'm not so great at it, so I'm thinking of taking up something else."

Officer Romero Alonso bent over until his eyes met Millicent's. "I wasn't such a fantastic policeman when I joined the force. Time made me better. It'll make you better, too."

"Maybe," Millicent said.

Officer Romero Alonso shrugged, then he turned to Herb, motioned with a nod at the bullies, and said, "Let's get these three over to the station."

"Before you do, may I have a word with them?" Millicent asked.

"Sure," Officer Romero Alonso said. "Make it quick, though. You can still catch Juanita's performance. I'm sorry I'll be missing it. Duty calls."

Millicent went over to the bullies, who were arguing with one another.

"I knew this was a stupid idea," Fletch grumbled and sniffled.

"Does this—*ah-choo*—mean we don't get to keep the bikes?" asked Pollywog.

Nina saw Millicent and sneezed. "Boy, are you gonna get it, Madding," she snarled. Looking away, she added, "as soon as I get out of juvenile detention."

Millicent studied Nina's scowling face. The bully seemed scared under her grim expression. Suddenly, Millicent wondered why she'd ever been frightened of Nina.

"What're you staring at?" Nina said.

"Nothing," Millicent said. "Absolutely nothing." She turned and walked back into the theater.

Twenty-five

Millicent found a seat in the rear of the theater just as the emcee announced the final performer of the afternoon, Juanita Romero Alonso. Millicent applauded as Juanita took to the stage. From the moment her bow hit the strings of her violin, Juanita had the audience so mesmerized they didn't even notice she was sniffling throughout the entire performance. During the crescendo, she *ah-ah-ahed*, but didn't actually sneeze. On her final note, though, she let out a sneeze so boisterous it shattered her otherwise ladylike image. She curtsied, trying to hide her nose.

Millicent gave Juanita a standing ovation, clapping so hard her palms turned red.

Millicent was sorry she'd missed Tonisha's poetry reading, and sorrier she hadn't seen Pollock's art on display in the theater lobby. She crossed her fingers for them, nonetheless.

After a few minutes of waiting while the judges conferred, the emcee approached the mic with a sheet of paper in his hand. He cleared his throat. "My," he said, "it's been something of an afternoon, hasn't it? We've had an imposter and three arrests." The audience murmured in response, and Millicent blushed. "But, now, for the part of the contest you came to see—the winners of this eventful competition."

"In the vocal competition," the emcee said. "The winner is—the *real* Iva Asimova for her rendition of 'Let Me Call You Sweetheart' . . . in *real* Czech." The audience voiced its approval as Iva accepted her award.

Millicent slumped in her seat, hoping no one would notice her.

The emcee announced the first runner-up in the spoken word category. Millicent clenched her fists as the contestant thanked the audience. "And the winner is—Tonisha Fontaine for her poem entitled, 'Fletchie.'"

A glowing Tonisha accepted her award, bowing so low that her headwrap pointed at the audience like a finger.

Millicent applauded crazily.

"Next, in the visual arts category, the first runner-up is—Everett Wong, whose work just barely made it to the lobby, where it is now on display."

Pollock went onstage, received his plaque, and took the microphone from the emcee. "It's Pollock," he said in a stuffy voice, "Pollock Wong. Thank you."

"For her fashion illustrations, the winner of the visual arts category is Fiona Dimmet of Pretty Liddy's Junior Fashion Academy," the emcee announced.

Pollock scrunched his nose as Fiona accepted her award.

The emcee revealed the first runner-up in the music category, a seven-year-old pianist. "Finally, the winner of the instrumental performance category is," the emcee said, "Juanita Romero Alonso, for her moving violin solo."

Juanita bounced onstage, accepted her plaque with a smile, and curtsied.

"Let's have a hand for all of our talented contestants!" the emcee said.

The audience gave a hearty round of applause. Millicent stood, clapping hard. One by one, the rest of the audience stood, while the winners joined hands and bowed.

The crowd eventually thinned to a small cluster of people congratulating Pollock, Tonisha, Juanita, and the other winners. Millicent hovered a few yards away, fiddling with the hem of her sweatshirt. She wanted to congratulate her friends, too, but kept her distance. They walked out to the front steps and sat down. Millicent followed them.

A hand rested on her shoulder. She spun around to see who it was.

"Leon! You're better!" she said.

"Pretty much," he said. "I caught your performance. Honestly, it was pretty bad. It kept me awake, though." He folded his arms. "Have you told them the truth, like I suggested?" He bobbed his head toward Pollock, Juanita, and Tonisha.

"Not really," Millicent answered. "In fact, I kind of made things worse."

Leon took her by the hand and tugged her. "But it's all over now, isn't it? You may as well come clean."

Millicent resisted slightly, then let Leon drag her toward her friends.

"Hi," she said, after a few seconds.

Pollock, Juanita, and Tonisha looked over their shoulders at her. "Hi," they said coolly. "Hi, Leon. Glad you're feeling better."

"Congratulations," Millicent said. "I'm proud of you guys."

"Thanks," Tonisha said.

"And?" Leon prompted.

Millicent sat next to her friends. She apologized immediately for all the trouble Bully-Be-Gone had caused. "I need to explain what happened," she said.

"Mmm-hmm," said Pollock, completely uninterested.

Juanita absentmindedly reached for her violin.

"Girl, all I can say is this had better be good." Tonisha

was the only one to look directly at Millicent.

Although they were tight-lipped, on the verge of bursting into rages, they listened quietly as she explained what had happened. She sighed and told them the reason the bullies had stolen their things and wanted to marry them was not because they really liked them. Bully-Be-Gone was too effective.

"We knew that," said Pollock.

"That's why we told you we believed something was wrong with it," said Juanita, wiping her nose with a tissue. "We knew."

"So what was that stuff you sprayed on them—on us?" Pollock asked.

"Hooky Spray. I invented it to clog their noses so they wouldn't be affected by Bully-Be-Gone," Millicent said. "Unfortunately, I couldn't see behind the curtain to aim properly. Sorry."

Tonisha seemed lost in thought. "I didn't know it was because of Bully-Be-Gone that Fletch—" she said quietly. "I thought he—"

Millicent glanced sidelong at Tonisha.

"I'm sorry, Tonisha," said Millicent. "Really, really sorry."

Tonisha pursed her lips and stared at the sidewalk. "He wouldn't have been half bad if he didn't have a criminal record," she said. She slapped Millicent playfully on the arm. "Just don't invent anything like that again."

They all laughed.

After a moment, things quieted down. Juanita started to chuckle and said, "Millicent, you're a lousy singer."

They laughed again. "Friends?" Millicent asked breathlessly.

"Friends," Pollock, Juanita, and Tonisha replied. Leon didn't say anything. He'd already dozed off.

"Then, if you'll excuse me," said Millicent, standing up. "I have to go home. Uncle Phineas must know by now that I took the Hooky Spray. It's time to pay the piper."

Twenty-six

A block away from her house, Millicent sat in her car, biting her bottom lip. A crowd of people milled about on her lawn. Some were in tight groups, talking. Just ahead of Millicent, a canary-yellow van was parked, a red KMVL logo printed on its broad side. A slogan was printed beneath the logo: "Wherever news is, you are, because we are where news is. And news is what it is because you are what you are. Therefore, where you are, we are, because where you are is news." Not the catchiest slogan, but it forced folks to watch the news just so they could try to decipher its meaning. A television crew, toting bulky, black video cameras, hovered like flies around Masonville's top television reporter and hair-spray spokesperson, KMVL's own Bonnie Fung.

"Now what did I do wrong?" Millicent asked herself. Considering the events of the past week, she assumed this current hullabaloo was linked to her.

She got out of her car and walked slowly, cautiously, toward her house.

She recognized some of the people on Uncle Phineas's lawn as the oddballs she saw running into town from the Curmudgeonly Mountains. The little twin boys were there with the woman in the gray uniform. The man with the briefcase chatted with the cowboy and the slender woman in the print dress. Bundled together in the background, they watched as Bonnie Fung prepared to interview the man in the pink leather suit.

"And in three, two, one," said a cameraman, counting down with his upheld fingers. Bonnie Fung removed a wad of gum from her mouth, stuck it behind her ear, and smoothed the lapels of her navy blue suit. The cameraman pointed to her.

"We're coming to you live from the home of a Phineas Baldernot," said Bonnie Fung, her expression newscaster serious, "where the survivors of a near-fatal brush with a bus crash and a wild bear are gathered. We're speaking with Boris Hoggle, survivor and unlikely hero of this averted tragedy."

"Hi," said Boris, waving to the camera.

206

"Were you frightened at all during your ordeal?" asked Bonnie Fung.

"Me?" asked Boris. "No. Nerves of steel." He puffed out his chest. "Get my good side," he said to the cameraman.

"I understand you carried a woman all the way down the Curmudgeonly Mountains on your back—and that you have a herniated disk. Wasn't that awfully painful?" the reporter asked into her microphone. Then she shoved it into Boris's face.

"I know not the meaning of pain when another's life is in danger," he replied. "I thought nothing of myself or my own maladies."

Millicent scowled. She distinctly recalled him saying something about terrible bayonets of affliction stabbing his back as he lumbered past her car.

"Does this mean I'm famous?" Boris asked Bonnie Fung.

"For at least fifteen minutes," said Bonnie.

"That's enough for me," said Boris.

"This is Bonnie Fung, reporting live from Masonville for KMVL news," said Bonnie, oozing with professionalism. Then she shouted, "Cut!"

Still confused as to why these people were gathered on her front lawn, Millicent wound her way through the crowd in search of Uncle Phineas. He deserved an apology. She'd find him and make amends. As she dodged people, she caught snippets of conversation, most of which contained the words, *bear*, *bus*, *cliff*, *crash*, and *ran*.

Under a maple tree, she saw Uncle Phineas with the old bride she'd seen on Boris's back. They were unaware of the commotion around them, as if the maple tree were their own private, canopied world. They held each other at arm's length. Why were they being so affectionate with each other? Who was the old bride? A tear cascaded down the woman's cheek. Uncle Phineas wiped it away, taking care not to smudge her makeup. Millicent thought the scene sentimental but very strange.

The bride reached into the pocket of her orange parka, producing a set of rings that appeared to be tiny bagels.

"Will you marry me again?" she asked.

Millicent inhaled and held her breath. *Oh my gosh.* Aunt Felicity! The human cannonball! No wonder she looked so familiar.

"We were never unmarried," Uncle Phineas pointed out. "Just the same, yes, I'll marry you again."

"These will have to do for now," said Felicity regretfully. She presented the tiny bagels on her quivering palm. "They're Engagement Bagel Rings. See? Rock salt diamonds."

"Perfection."

Uncle Phineas let her slip the snack jewelry on his finger. They embraced for several moments and Uncle Phineas rested his head on his wife's shoulder, his eyes closed.

For the first time in days, Millicent was happy. Next to getting her parents back, this was the best gift she could imagine.

Uncle Phineas opened one eye and saw his niece.

"Millicent," he said, "thank you."

"I'm s-s-s-sorry," Millicent said, feeling the weight of the Hooky Spray in her pocket.

Uncle Phineas smiled. "Thank you."

"I'm giving up inventing and—" said Millicent.

"Thank you," said Uncle Phineas.

"I know w-what I did was wrong," Millicent stuttered. "And— What did you say?"

"I said thank you."

"But I did a bad thing."

"If you're speaking of taking the Hooky Spray and attending an after-school function without my permission—" Uncle Phineas said.

Millicent squinted, ready for her punishment.

"All is forgiven," Uncle Phineas continued.

Millicent gave him a bewildered look.

Together, Uncle Phineas and Felicity told her the whole story of how they believed they were reunited. Uncle Phineas told how he had applied his old cologne, Strong Like Bull, and Bully-Be-Gone in liberal doses. Felicity told how her memory had returned when the beautiful smells of her life rained upon her in the park. Piecing their fragments of stories together, they had come to the conclusion that Bully-Be-Gone traveled all the way to Pinnimuk City, where it had awakened Aunt Felicity's memory. There was, they said, no other explanation.

"I don't know the hows and whys and wherefores of this

miracle," said Uncle Phineas. "It is my theory, though, that you have brought my Felicity back to me." He clasped Felicity's hand between his, as if he feared she might get away if he let go.

Millicent was speechless. Was their reunion Bully-Be-Gone's doing, or was it a fluke of galactic proportions? Or was it both?

"My dear child," said Felicity, "say 'you're welcome.'"

Taking credit was like a pair of uncomfortable shoes for Millicent, after all she'd been through. Accustomed to taking blame, yet intrigued that, perhaps, this stroke of for-tuitousness had something to do with her, she scratched her head. Why not? She'd give accepting merit a try. She put her hands on her hips and said, "Okay. Okay. You're welcome." Saying it felt good. Great. She cocked her head to one side. She could get used to this. She said it again. "You're welcome." Then she shouted it. "You're welcome!"

Felicity laughed. Uncle Phineas slapped his knee.

Millicent beamed. Maybe she'd been a bit hasty in vowing to quit inventing. If this was the accidental out-come of her handiwork, then imagine what she could accomplish on purpose!

Twenty-seven

Millicent, Uncle Phineas, and Aunt Felicity sat on the front porch for a long time that evening, talking over lemonade and tea and cake. Millicent told them about everything—her friends, the bullies, and their stolen bikes.

When she mentioned that she had considered giving up her career as an inventor, Uncle Phineas shook his head and told her that he was glad she changed her mind. "I have always had faith in you, dear niece," he said. He took a sip of tea. "Besides, your parents would be proud, yes? Yes."

"I should think so," Aunt Felicity said, using her free

hand to dab the corner of her mouth with a napkin. Her other hand hadn't let go of Uncle Phineas's since they'd been reunited.

"I think so, too." Millicent admired the stars set far away in the night sky. She picked out two that shined brighter than hope and imagined they were her mother and father. The pair of stars pulsed as if speaking to her in Morse code. *We are so very proud of you,* they seemed to be saying. Millicent closed her eyes. She could almost hear them talking to her. *So very proud.* A warm feeling caressed her heart.

Uncle Phineas poured himself and Aunt Felicity another cup of tea. As he stirred in some sugar his spoon hit the sides of his cup and broke the silence.

Millicent opened her eyes, the warmth in her heart spreading to her stomach like hot chocolate.

"This thing about bullies," Uncle Phineas began.

"What about them?" Millicent asked.

"They've been around for all of recorded history," he said. "I think evolution put them here to test our mettle. Yes. If we've nothing to fear, we've nothing to become."

"Are you saying there's nothing we can do about them?" she asked.

"No, I didn't say that." He chuckled.

"What are you saying?" she asked.

"I'm not sure, exactly," he said. "But, to use an aquatic illustration, yes, I'm reminded of the humble blowfish who, when sensing the threat of attack, inflates himself to an unmanageable size."

"I don't get it," said Millicent.

"Yes. I don't know that I do either," he said. "But I think the answer lies in becoming more of yourself in the presence of bullies, not less."

More of myself, Millicent thought.

They talked for a while longer and were about to call it a night when a small figure approached in the dim evening light.

"Millicent," a voice said. "I've been searching everywhere for you."

Roderick. He trotted up the walkway, his hands behind his back. He was dressed up, wearing neatly pressed trousers, a white shirt, and a bow tie. Millicent cringed. If she were a betting kind of gal, she'd wager he was dressed for dinner. Pizza, to be precise.

"We should take our leave," said Uncle Phineas, winking at Aunt Felicity. "We've dishes to wash and much catching up to do, yes?"

Aunt Felicity smiled. "A stack of dishes and years of catching up."

"Please don't," begged Millicent in a hoarse whisper.

"Good night, dear niece," Uncle Phineas said, arching an eyebrow in Millicent's direction. He rose from the porch and helped Aunt Felicity up. Aunt Felicity bent down and kissed the top of Millicent's head, then they both went inside the house, the screen door snapping shut behind them.

Roderick hopped onto the first porch step. "I brought

you these," he said, presenting her with a bouquet of flowers from his yard.

She took them, biting her tongue.

"Uh, thank you?" She didn't mean for it to sound like a question, but it came out sounding like one.

"Eat'cha Pizza is still open," Roderick hinted. "It's pizza-my-heart night." He sat on the step next to her.

"Is it?" she asked, scooting away.

Up close and under a pool of moonlight, Roderick didn't look half bad. He'd slicked his hair up into little spikes and his breath smelled like peppermint. Millicent thought she might be able to tolerate a meal with him—*might*.

"What do you say?" Roderick asked. "Pizza? With *moi*?"

Millicent had been to Eat'cha Pizza a few times. She found the atmosphere entertaining. You were given 3-D glasses with which to watch the dinner tables. Three dimensional movies of Mama Giovanni, the pizza parlor's owner, ran nonstop on the tabletops under your plate. "Eat'cha pizza, eat'cha pizza! You look too skinny! *Prego, prego*," Mama Giovanni's image shouted repeatedly as you tried to scarf down your food. Millicent thought it might be distraction enough from dining with Roderick. She might actually enjoy eating with him. She glanced again at his swooning face. Then again, maybe not.

"I don't know . . ." Millicent mused aloud.

Roderick leaned toward her, and the secret chamber key he wore around his neck—the very key that had been handed down through generations of the Madding clan—

214

swung like a pendulum. She stared at it, not uttering a word.

"My treat," said Roderick, breaking the silence. "I mean, I *am* rich. My father *is* an attorney and my mother *is* president and CEO of Beauty Goo Cosmetics, you know." Millicent winced. He rotated his shoulders back so that his chest bulged, then grinned at her. "Besides, isn't that what boys do? Treat you girls to pizza?"

Millicent gasped. Girls could, just as easily, treat boys to pizza. Evidently, even Bully-Be-Gone couldn't erase Roderick's huge ego, much less his chauvinistic attitude. And "chauvinist" was just another word for a boy bully.

She tried to recall the point Uncle Phineas tried to make with his blowfish example. What was she that she could become more of in the presence of bullies? "Clever" was the sole adjective that came to mind. Slyly, she took something out of her pocket, turned her back on Roderick, and pretended to smell the flowers he'd brought.

"What are you squirting on those flowers?" asked Roderick.

She turned to face him again.

"Uh . . . a sort of smell enhancer I invented," she said, her face flushed. "Yeah . . . Magna-Sniff, I call it. Mmm-hmm. Magna-Sniff." Uncle Phineas was right. This becoming more of yourself was fun. "Think of it as . . . uh . . . a magnifying glass for your nose," she added for good measure. She thrust the bouquet at him. "Here. Smell 'em."

"I've already smelled them," he said. "They're from my own yard."

"Smell 'em again," said Millicent, fanning the bouquet in his face.

"Nah," said Roderick. "I know what they smell like."

"Pleeeease," she said, batting her eyelashes as she'd seen Tonisha do. "Please—honey."

Roderick's face sparkled. "I'll gladly partake of your invention," he said. "I'm sure nature's fragrance is made doubly delicious through your ingenuity." He took the bouquet, nestled his nose in its petals, and sucked in a lungful of scent.

Millicent handed him a hanky as he began to sniffle. "I think you'll be needing this."

She giggled to herself and, overhead, two stars seemed to giggle in return.